REALM OF BEASTS

LEGEND OF THE NAMELESS ONE: BOOK ONE

ANGELA J. FORD

The Four Worlds Series

The Complete Four Worlds Series (Books 1–4)

The Five Warriors

The Blended Ones

Myran: A Tale of the Four Worlds

Eliesmore and the Green Stone

Eliesmore and the Jeweled Sword

Legend of the Nameless One

Citrine's Monsters: Prequel to Legend of the Nameless One

Realm of Beasts

To the fans of the Four Worlds.

CONTENTS

REALM OF MORTALS

SUMMER. YEAR 965.
LAND OF LOCK. THE SOUTH WORLD.

WHO AM I?

Where did I come from?

What is my name?

Three questions buzzed around his head like vultures over a fresh kill as he crept toward the gut-wrenching smell. His nose wrinkled. A rotten scent wafted through the air, ruining the pleasant flavors of nature with the stench of death. His pulse pounded as he crawled through the golden-yellow grass waving above his head, his movements silent like the wild cats that stalked the forest and open lands.

If you want to know who you are and where you came from, go to Daygone.

The words rang in his memory as if it were yesterday.

Ten years ago, he had said goodbye to the green giantess who raised him and spoke those words. He knew she was not a giant, but that's how he preferred to think of her, for her true name was a harbinger of death. The word *Daygone* rang in his head like a bad omen—a place where dreams went to die. A darkness flashed in the giant's eyes when she said the word. *Daygone.* He could almost detect the bitter mystery that turned rotten, much like the scent he breathed now.

He twitched his nose as a swarm of gnats rose, droning around his face as if fighting an invisible war with one who dared invade their haven of grass. Pausing on all fours, he took a deep breath, fighting back the sneeze until it erupted out of his throat. *Ka-choom!*

A guilty cough followed as he glanced around, scanning the green meadow with his dark eyes to see if he had disturbed anyone.

An ear-splitting screech made him jump as a flock of buzzards rose in the air, flapping their dark wings and screaming at each other. Torn bits of flesh hung from their claws and blood covered their beaks. He squinted. Whatever kill they were devouring had been dead for a few days.

"Torrrrrr Lir . . ." A sing-song voice called in warning and a creature pounced on him, knocking him flat on his back. He grunted in annoyance as the creature sat on his torso, pinning him down while pounding on his chest.

"Why did you leave?" she demanded, poking him none too gently. "It took me days to find you. If I wasn't skilled in tracking, I might not have found you at all." The liquid-gold eyes of the female Jesnidrain moved with animation as she scolded him and jabbed his ribs with her sharp fingernails.

"Lelia." He cut her off abruptly as he held up both hands in surrender. He felt peeved she'd been able to find him so quickly. "What are you doing out here? You're not supposed to leave the forests of Shimla."

The five-foot-tall creature paused mid-sentence and a swift look of anger came over her heart-shaped face. Her jeweled eyes narrowed and her pointed ears turned red as they quivered. "You can leave, but I can't?"

"I am not an Iaen." Tor Lir trailed off as Lelia scowled down at him. Her nose twitched, yet she looked lovely, glaring down at him while smelling of the jasmine gardens of Shimla. Giving into weakness, he let his thoughts drift, inhaling her scent and enjoying the warmth of her body pressed against his. Her pert breasts stood out and if he reached out a hand, he could squeeze them and rub his face between them as he'd done often in the past.

"You *are* an Iaen," Lelia insisted, emphasizing her words with one last jab. "Besides, if you can leave Shimla, so can I."

He propped his upper body on his elbows, slightly dislodging the Jesnidrain. Keeping his expression calm, he attempted to explain. "But you cannot come with me. It could be dangerous."

"You lie." Her anger dissolved into laughter. "What

could be dangerous in *this* world? There is nothing to fear." She wriggled her hips, clutching his body with her thighs as if he were a horse.

"You don't know and neither do I," he disagreed, ignoring her attempt at foreplay. He was strong enough to leave the seduction of the Iaens of Shimla once, and he would do so again. "It's our first time leaving the shelter of Shimla, a world within worlds. We don't know what it's like out here in the realm of mortals."

"Why are you out here in the realm of mortals?" She crossed her arms over her chest, her ruby lips drawn down into a frown.

He sat up, sliding her further off his body. He moved his face closer until their noses were mere inches apart. "You know why I have to go. I am the balancer of good and evil. The past twenty years were calm, but I sense the seeds of unrest have sprouted. Where there is mischief, I must restore the balance. Where there is need, it is unsafe. You cannot come with me. You are not strong enough."

"But you are." All the same, the Jesnidrain's words came out sullen as she met his gaze and tilted her head, begging for a kiss. "You can protect me."

"Not if the balance calls for death. It's best to stay away. If peace comes and I can return, I will." He kept his tone solemn as he looked her in the eye, neither moving nor blinking.

After a moment, Lelia shivered and stood. Backing away from him, she rubbed her hands over her bare arms. Her straight black hair swished around her waist and the intoxicating scent of jasmine faded.

He studied her, examining her lithe form as he waited for the truth to sink into her mind. When he was young, he'd noted the uncanny vibe he gave off. It was an aura of cool aloofness. When he slowed down his words and stared into someone's eyes, they felt cold like the breath of an icy winter coming for them. The first time he'd used the odd power was on the green giantess, and occasionally he used it when the minor annoyances of the Iaens—the immortal creatures of Shimla—grew too alluring. He already regretted trysting with Lelia the Jesnidrain. In the future, he would control his urges lest a flock of unwanted females followed wherever he went.

"I will walk with you until nightfall," Lelia decided, her steady voice leaving no room for questions.

He shrugged, torn between conflicting feelings. Lelia was a slight seductress in her own way, but she was smart and her company was not completely unwelcome. Turning his back to her, he took a few steps forward. "Do you smell that?"

The corners of Lelia's mouth turned down and the perfect skin in between her brows creased into wrinkles. "It smells foul . . ." She trailed off and strode forward while the grasses parted for her muscular calves.

He eyed her and followed a few paces behind.

She slowed down as she reached the spot where the buzzards had flown. Tilting his head, Tor Lir spotted the birds circling above, waiting for peace so they could return to their interrupted meal.

A high-pitched shriek jerked his head back down. Lelia stood rigid, frozen in terror as she screamed. Tor Lir watched her with lidded eyes, keeping the smirk from crossing his face while the words *I warned you* danced on the edge of his lips. Genuine horror made Lelia's face red as the beets that grew on the outskirts of Shimla while her round eyes looked as if they would pop.

When her first fright had passed, she spun around. Eyes blazing, she stalked back to him with her hands on her hips. Scorn was written across her face and her jaw tightened as she glared up at him. Before he could react, she lifted a hand with lightning speed and slapped his cheek. The sound rang out, echoing across the quiet meadow. His hand flew to his face, more surprised than hurt at her reaction.

"I've always known you were full of tricks!" She spewed her words at him. "You play with power and make sure everything that happens is according to your desires, but this is too far! I am done with you, Tor Lir of Shimla. You are no longer welcome in my Jasmine Gardens and I'll make sure every Jesnidrain knows to stay away from you."

Tor Lir snorted as she marched away, spreading the thin wings on her back, gaining speed. Although she had wings, she couldn't fly. Her kind lived with a misfortune. Some of them had the ability of flight while others did not. He supposed she meant her words to be damaging, but he felt grateful the danger in the realm of mortals turned out to be true. No longer would he be saddled with her delicious yet annoying company. He made a note to be careful who he had sex with, for beauty and pleasure were fleeting.

Free of distractions, he strutted over to gaze at the dead creature the buzzards had been eating. The sight made his blood run cold, and he took a step backward, almost tripping over his own feet.

A male lay headlong in the grass. Dark sockets where his eyes used to be gazed at the cloudless sky while clotted blood covered his body. His flesh was in various stages of decay due to the warmth and new blood that spurted from the holes where the buzzards pecked away.

Death was a word he knew yet had never seen, and revulsion shook his body. It was clear something killed the male in a ruthless and painful manner and then left him to rot. His soul would have trouble passing to the Beyond without a proper burial. Thoughts swirled through Tor Lir's mind.

Who did this?

Where are they?

Why?

2

A STIR OF DRAMA

THE FRAGRANCE OF WHITE LOTUS HUNG HEAVY in the air. Novor Tur-Woodberry knelt in the warm soil, examining the gray vines worming through the bright garden of marigolds and poppies. A cluster of gray weeds grew up around the base of the flowers, threatening to choke the life out. They hissed as he tossed them aside and patted the rich dirt back down so the vivid yellow and dark-red flowers could blossom. The low melody of bumblebees hummed around him and he stood, surveying his handiwork and stretching his broad shoulders in the sunlight.

A nearby oak tree reached its lengthy boughs toward him, inviting him into the shade. A wide smile covered his bearded face as he nodded in acknowledgment. Taking a deep breath of the scented air, he felt a potent sense of peace. For the first time in hundreds of years, there was no nagging suspicion that a great evil would befall the world. The troublesome vines in his flower garden seemed a brief nuisance considering the calamity that had overcome the world the past one hundred years.

"Novor Tur-Woodberry! Novor Tur-Woodberry!" an exhilarated voice shouted from below.

"Oy!" Novor Tur-Woodberry rumbled, his dark-blue eyes spying the creature that moved in a blur through the grass. The gift of speech blessed more than half the creatures in the South World. His land teemed with life, speech, and the constant sound of music echoing off the rolling green hills of Locherenixzes. It was a true Paradise where the plants, animals, and mortals dwelt in peace and harmony without fear. Now and then, a disagreement or minor unpleasantness would arise, causing a stir of drama and gossiping tongues, until Novor Tur-Woodberry scolded everything into its place. Often, new inhabitants caused discord, but it had been at least ten years since the last seeds of calamity swept across the land. Novor Tur-Woodberry was content to let the peace continue.

"Novor Tur-Woodberry, there's trouble!" A black weasel with patches of white fur stood on his hind legs, his whiskers quivering and his nose moving as he spoke.

"Not on my land." Novor Tur-Woodberry chuckled. "Come along, show me."

"This way." The weasel went on, dropping to all fours and making rivets through the grass. The green way parted before them as they moved northeast. "I was foraging for food. I have babies, you know. And the wife need not be out in the wild, looking for food."

"Nor need you," Novor Tur-Woodberry said. "My Fúlishités will bring you any provision you need. What with a new family, you must be hard-pressed to find enough food."

The weasel gave a squeak and paused, twitching his nose as he eyed Novor Tur-Woodberry, a sheepish expression coming over his face. "Don't tell the wife, will you? I need time away from the litter to run wild. Food is my only excuse."

"Aye, your secret is safe with me." Novor Tur-Woodberry winked at the weasel, eyes twinkling. "Carry on with your tale."

"Where was I?" the weasel asked himself as he leaped forward, leading the way once again. "Ah. On my way, I bumped into Toad, who was headed down to the marshes. I don't know what he was doing out in the pastures, but he claimed the dragonflies lured him out."

"Dragonflies," Novor Tur-Woodberry mused, turning the word over on his tongue. "Aye, they usually stay by the marshes. What are they doing out here in the grasslands?"

The weasel stood upright and held its tiny paws up to the sky. "I did not consider it odd the dragonflies were out, not until Toad showed me what I'm about to show you."

Novor Tur-Woodberry stroked his beard, an old habit. As a powerful Duneíthaír, trouble ceased to worry him after the war between the mortals and immortals ended. There was no one left to stand against him. "Have you showed anyone else?"

"Nay. I searched for the Fúlishités first, but they must be in the northern reaches of the land."

"Oh ho," Novor Tur-Woodberry rumbled. His Fúlishités were a tribe of ten little men, often called Singing Men, for they roamed the land, singing of the legendary greatness of Novor Tur-Woodberry while helping him tend the land. They were happy and loyal and often stuck together, their voices carrying through the air when they came upon something Novor Tur-Woodberry needed to investigate. "Wait." Novor Tur-Woodberry held up a finger and sniffed as a new scent entered his land. He noticed the familiar tug of excitement, almost as if someone had walked across an invisible portal and triggered an alarm. "There is someone new in the land," he told the weasel.

"Must you go to them?"

"Nay, let's explore the lagoon and then I will visit them. I believe they will be amenable."

"No one new has come here since the Tider with the odd eyes," the weasel pointed out, his tail bouncing behind him as he jumped.

"Citrine." Novor Tur-Woodberry nodded fondly. The curious young female held a strange aura, yet she'd been living on his land the past three months without mishap and all who met her accepted her. "Usually we have more visitors. The land is at peace. The people groups settle and rebuild, yet I expect more Crons will come through this land, seeking adventure and knowledge."

"Almost there," the weasel called out, in a haste to get back to his family. "The wife will wonder why I've been gone for so long."

A snake hissed as they neared the marshes and blue dragonflies scattered overhead. A fog rolled over the lagoon and the weasel paused, its nose quivering as it pointed a shaking paw. "Have you seen this before?"

A darkness spread beyond the marshes, and the ground changed from nasty brown into black, like a fever of poison spreading. Novor Tur-Woodberry crossed his arms, frowning as his eyes took in the sight, and his senses alerted him to a deeper knowledge he'd long forgotten. At length, he turned back to the weasel. "Go home to your family. Leave me to worry about this."

"Aye." The weasel waited for Novor Tur-Woodberry's low rumble of laughter, but as there was none forthcoming, it turned and scampered off.

Alone, Novor Tur-Woodberry squinted and surveyed the land. A blue dragonfly flew above him, the gentle hum of its delicate voice drifting through the stale air. "Novor Tur-Woodberry. What is the blackness? Is it death?"

"When did you first see it?" Tur-Woodberry asked the dragonfly, noting its brilliant wings that buzzed ceaselessly back and forth.

"Hum . . . ho . . . a week or so."

"You did not tell me?" he asked without blame, for

the land was odd and did not always require his attention.

"Hum . . ." The dragonfly buzzed. "We thought it would go away, and then it didn't, so we told Toad. It wasn't this bad before. Are you going to fix it? Isn't the blackness trespassing on your land?"

Novor Tur-Woodberry stroked his beard. "It is. I will inspect the borders."

3

SUNSHINE AT LAST

CITRINE PRESSED THE HERBS TO HER NOSE AND spread them across the table. She stroked their vines and leaves, one by one, as if she were their lover. Enticing scents imbued the air, securing the soulful bond between herself and nature. Leaning over, she eyed the instructions on the parchment held open by a gray rock and a white candle. Three key ingredients were missing from her concoction. Perhaps the gardens near the Standing Stones had the plants she sought. She stood. Humming.

> *"A spell of protection. A spell of disguise.*
> *A spell to hide from prying eyes.*
> *A spell of deflection. A spell of desire.*
> *A spell to hide from seeking eyes."*

A wave of guilt made her shudder, and she rubbed her arms together. Golden sunbeams flickered over her worktable, reminding her that time was passing. Three months she'd hidden, working in what seemed to be Paradise. A glorious haven that belonged to a friendly giant called Novor Tur-Woodberry. Tossing her cutting knife down, she huffed in frustration as she moved to the bed. It was taking too long for her to recall the spell. Too long to find the memories that took her back. She needed to rewrite the book of spells, but safety and protection for her beasts were top of mind. Turning over blankets, she searched for the yellow scarf she used to carry herbs and flowers.

Tying the handkerchief around her waist, she flung open the door and hurried out. A gentle breeze made goosebumps stand up on her bare arms. Rolling green hills seemed as if they moved up and down, like waves on the shore. Despite her conflicted feelings, golden light surrounded her and its buoyancy calmed her. Spreading her arms wide, she breathed in the glorious air while the sound of delicate music danced by her ears on the breeze.

"Sunshine at last," she whispered.

The past week, it had rained in the glorious land of Novor Tur-Woodberry and although it was a delicious rain, she missed the sunshine all the same. A smile came to her face as she recalled the relief she felt at being welcomed by Novor Tur-Woodberry and the peaceful people of the land. It was hard to believe she did not dwell in the realm of the immortals, although she had forsaken her beasts. A frown broke the smile on her face. She'd promised her beasts a home. Instead of bringing them with her, she entered Paradise alone. She chewed on her bottom lip and played with the frayed ends of her handkerchief.

The emerald-green hills rolled as she walked, holding a hand out as if she could touch the grace and beauty in the air. A sprouting oak tree grew just outside her cottage, and she walked up to it, placing a hand on its slim trunk. "Are you home?" she whispered. "Your roots are growing strong, drinking in the rainwater—come out and see, sunshine is here."

A silvery shimmer came over the air. The tree moved, stretching its small branches until it seemed as if the tree were a mirror and there were two trees, breathing in the golden light.

"Citrine," a high voice called and suddenly there were two trees no more. A green Trespiral—the spirit of the tree—appeared, standing with willowy grace as it beamed at Citrine.

She reached out a hand in awe, twirling as the Trespiral caught her fingers in one of its branches and spun her around.

"I feel refreshed and anew, but I must go back inside to grow while the sunshine is here," the Trespiral admitted.

"You've grown since the rain. There's silver on your branches, and I see new buds."

The Trespiral laughed, a silvery tinkle that matched the underlying cadence of music across the land.

"Will you tell me your name?" Citrine asked. "We talk each day, but I still don't know your name."

The Trespiral's bark-brown skin stood out in contrast to the golden light. Leaf-green hair trailed around her shoulders. "I am too young for a name. When I am older and understand my purpose, then my name shall be revealed."

"Is that the custom of trees? They give us mortals our names a few days after birth. Name day is what we call it."

A tranquil breeze drifted across the grassy hillock and the Trespiral swayed in it as if it were the beginning of a dance. "Mortals are reckless with names. Immortals understand the potency of giving a name to another."

Citrine snorted. "It's not that important." She sobered at the Trespiral's indignant expression. "I only meant . . . your ways differ greatly from mine. I am not making fun, merely seeking to understand."

"I can feel wafts of knowledge drifting past me, which is why I say what I do. Tell me, do you know your purpose?"

A memory flashed through Citrine's mind. White bone. Dark eyes. The smell of death. Guilt gnawed at her core, reminding her of the promise she'd made but hadn't fulfilled. Serenity drained from her face, replaced with a flash of anger. "Yes." Her tone came out flat. "Right now, I am going to the Standing Stones to gather herbs."

"Ah, I see I have made you unhappy. No one should be unhappy in the land of Novor Tur-Woodberry. Go. Forget my words. Find joy."

"I am not unhappy," Citrine protested. "Memories of my life before I came here are not pleasant. Enjoy growing. I'll come to visit you during the moonlight when you have more time."

"The realm of night," the Trespiral whispered as she sank back into the tree, closing her eyes to meditate and grow.

Citrine continued up the invisible path that curved back and forth over the hills, leading into the heights. At one high point, she saw stone cottages with thatched roofs dotting the hillsides. The wild and tame animals of the land gazed in peace, moving from the hilltop to the valley to find the greenest grass. Following the path, she reached the pond with the well beside it where she drew fresh water for baking. She waved at the long-legged pink birds. Lily pads floated in the water, nosed aside by curved beaks as the birds hunted for the tiny fish. They nodded at her in acknowledgment, their beady eyes focused and intent.

Leaving the pond behind, she continued to climb until a flowing stream appeared, singing a quiet song.

Orange koi as big as her face with great whiskers swam through the crystal-clear waters. Green roads and vine-covered bridges rose before her, showing off the enchantment of the land of Novor Tur-Woodberry. Flowers added bright colors to the lush greenery of the land—red roses, orange marigolds, white lotuses, red poppies, and violet irises. Citrine allowed herself a brief smile as she held her hands over the waving grass that came up to her waist. Despite her contentment with the land of Novor Tur-Woodberry, she found an unsettled restlessness growing within her. Three months and she'd found a home, and it wasn't enough.

Citrine.

A voice filtered through her thoughts. It was not the voice she expected, and she felt something within her stiffen. It was not fear, only respect, and a quiet peace rose as she replied. *Morag.* And waited.

The Master of the Forest has a request.

Citrine froze, one foot hovering in midair. The Master of the Forest was a dark creature and, in her anger, she'd made a deal she assumed was meaningless. That was before she'd come to this land and found people she cared about. Narrowing her eyes, although Morag was far from her, she replied. *I thought the Master of the Forest did not want to see me again.*

The Master of the Forest requested your presence in the Boundary Line Forest. You will not meet with him.

Citrine gave an exasperated sigh and her fingers twitched, yanking at the frayed ends of her handkerchief.

She wore a short dress, improper compared to the long skirts most females wore. However, she preferred the freedom to move her legs versus the modesty and fashion of present time. She frowned. Suddenly, the birds singing in the distance and the blue skies seemed to laugh at her plight. For a moment, she wished it were raining. *Morag, I thought you were in my service. You belong to me, not the Master of the Forest.*

Ignoring the Master of the Forest will make life in the woods difficult for me. If you care about me, you will do as requested.

I do not respond to threats! You are strong and powerful. What can the Master of the Forest do to you?

That is a question you know the answer to. You have seen the Master of the Forest and you continued to flee until you found sanctuary. You made a promise to us. Paradise. Will you fulfill that promise?

A flash of annoyance and anger came over Citrine and she bit her lip, her hands trembling. *Dare you throw my words back at me? The promises I make, I keep. Tell me, when and where does the Master wish for me to appear?*

This evening in the glade, just past twilight, something is waiting for you there.

Will I see you?

Do you wish to?

Of course, my quarrel is not with you. I will summon Ava, Zaul, and Grift.

My lady.

The threads of communication snapped and left Citrine alone, scowling at the bluebells in the wild green grass. Thoughts of a past life rose before her. Chocolate-brown eyes. A cottage in a village. A garden filled with herbs. A keen longing and a deep sorrow rose in her heart. Instead of giving in to the emotions, her scowl deepened and she marched across the land, smashing the grass with each footfall.

4

MORTAL FEARS

A MENACING GROWL SWEPT OVER THE MEADOW and the sudden overwhelming smell of rot wafted through the air. Tor Lir took a step back from the decaying body, covering his nose and mouth as the sulfuric smell grew. His eyes shifted, taking in the grass-covered rolling hills, and a muted-gray blur in the distance, a forest.

Turning around, he eyed the meadow, searching for life. In the distance, he thought he could see the quickly retreating form of Lelia as she headed back to Shimla. The past seven days, he'd walked through a haze of greenery in scenery different from his homeland, Shimla. A vague sensation tickled his thoughts with a truth he did not want to decipher. Faint words echoed in the back of his mind, words that grew stronger the longer he stayed in Shimla. *Long may you live. Long may you prosper.* A foreboding sat deep within him and he brushed it away, jolting out of dark possibilities as the growl came again, louder this time. Tor Lir stepped away from the body toward the gray wood, keeping his emerald eyes wide, watching for the creature roaming the green meadow.

A sniff with a prolonged, snorting bellow made the grass quiver. The meadow beneath Tor Lir's feet shook as a creature he could not see yet thundered toward him. Unsure what to do or how to handle incidents in the realm of mortals, he stood his ground, though he had no weapons.

In the forest of Shimla, Iaens brought creatures to reason with a show of aggression. They were wild through and through, their tempers rising and falling without a sense of normality. When disputes broke out, it was the strong who won.

Balling up his fists, Tor Lir gritted his teeth and prepared to show his dominance, yet the creature that appeared from the grasslands made him regret his choice. He should have run as soon as he heard the growl.

A monstrous beast clamored toward him on four short legs. Its body was low-lying like a reptile and a protective, tough, green hide covered its back. It had a long snout where a row of white curved fangs stuck out from its mouth. The creature moved with surprising speed through the waving grass, shattering the serenity of the prairie. Tor Lir stuck out a hand, palm facing the beast as if imploring it to stop. A lump formed in his throat as he realized how ill-equipped he was to deal with beasts in the realm of mortals.

At the last moment, the beast turned its body and swung its outstretched tail toward Tor Lir's legs. The tail smacked into his knees with such force it tossed him into the air. He gasped as the wind left his body and he fell heavily on his side, sending a jolting pain rocketing through his arm. Starlight marred his vision and when he could see again, the creature lay in wait a few feet away, as if egging him on, encouraging him to stand again.

Intelligent dark eyes flickered at him. The yawning mouth with a row of glittering teeth opened as the beast snapped at him. A growl bellowed out of its belly and shattered the pure air with the reek of sulfur and rot.

Choking on the horrific smell, Tor Lir clasped a hand over his nose as he stumbled to his feet. Trying to calm his rising panic, he backed away from the creature with one hand out. A knowledge settled in his core and internal alarm bells rang. He had nowhere to run. His goal would be to see how long he could stay alive before turning into the creature's next meal, for surely this was the beast that killed the male, turning him into a rotting corpse.

A thought flickered through Tor Lir's mind. *The Dance of the Dead.* If he could block and dodge the creature's attack, eventually he would wear it out and perhaps he could find safety in the woods. Throwing his head over his shoulder, he took the risk to glance behind, gauging how far the forest was. The beast took advantage of his moment of weakness and charged.

"Wait!" A cry flew from Tor Lir's lips as the beast leaped up and slammed into his stomach with his snout, flinging Tor Lir through the air.

Searing pain surged through his stomach from the sucker punch, and he crumpled into a ball—even as he flew, his face contorted in pain. *Misery. The realm of mortals is pure misery.*

A pressure built in his head as if powerful jaws were clamping down on him and through a blur of darkness, he felt his body being dragged through the grasslands. As soon as he regained air, he stuck his feet out and kicked, hindering the process somewhat. The last thing he needed was for the beast to drag him back to some lair, likely to be dinner for its offspring who would rip him to shreds alive.

Lifting his arms, he reached for the thing clamping down on his head and was rewarded with sharp teeth sinking into his flesh. He snatched his hand away, yelping. A quick glance showed the bite was not deep and only drew a thin trickle of blood.

"Let me go," he cried out. "I have no quarrel with you!"

The pressure disappeared and Tor Lir sat up, spinning around on his haunches in one fluid movement. The creature stood before him at eye level with its rounded snout open. Its black eyes blinked once, then twice, and the yawning mouth opened. Because of his close view, Tor Lir saw chunks of rotten meat in the beast's mouth while the fangs that stuck out were curved and sharp with hints of redness on them. Tor Lir noticed, with some trepidation, one fang was missing, leaving a bloody gap. Something trickled down his face, and he realized it was blood from where the creature had gripped him in its jaws.

Holding out both hands, palms up, Tor Lir crawled backward on his knees. From the corners of his eyes, he saw the gray forest was closer than before. With a burst of speed and luck, he might be able to reach it before the creature attacked again.

The beast did not move as he backed away, and slowly Tor Lir rose higher until he was on his feet once more, his body bruised and shaken from the beating he'd taken. Keeping his eye on the creature, he moved sideways toward the forest while decay drifted away and a pure wind blew. The musty smell of pine and old wood drifted past his face. His nose wrinkled as his eyes watered, but when he took a deep breath, he almost doubled over from the pain in his stomach. He squeezed his eyes shut to dull the sensation of agony. When he opened them again, the beast was running toward him, growling as its eyes lit up in glee. It was in that moment Tor Lir realized the beast was just playing with him. Death was inevitable. He lifted his legs, turned his back to the beast, and ran toward the forest as fast as he dared.

His sides ached as he fled, his feet tearing through

the grass, chunks of mud spraying out behind him. His heart thumped in his chest and his throat felt raw and ragged. The gray forest, which had seemed so close, now seemed miles away, as if it were taunting him. Balling up his fists, he willed himself faster while a mixture of sweat and blood poured down his head. Adrenaline surged through him and, when he saw the dark coolness of the forest, the creature slammed into him from behind. The tail wiped around, slammed the back of his feet, and Tor Lir fell headlong, smacking his head into the trunk of a tree.

A cry rose on his lips, forgotten as teeth closed around his ankle and he lost himself to the grip of oblivion.

5

THE STORYTELLER

THE AIR GREW COOL AND CRISP AS CITRINE approached the Standing Stones. She sighed, letting the unhappy news drift into the past. She'd worry about the message that evening, when she ventured into the forest again. For now, she let herself relax as she observed the audience gathered at the Stones.

Triften the Storyteller sat cross-legged on a boulder in front of the three waterfalls. The dull roar carried his voice across the churning cascades, amplifying his words to those who listened. Kai, the miller's daughter, sat at his feet, her hair the color of sunshine. She was soaking wet as the waterfall's spray danced around her. The attempts of the sunshine to dry her off were a laughing failure. Citrine smiled, reminded of herself when she was young and impulsive. The children of the village gathered around Triften. They were young, only five or six, their cheeks still round with baby fat, their eyes wide and innocent.

Five. That's how old Citrine was when the war ended. Memories of her younger years were vague, mapped with emotions. The joy on her parents' faces when they learned the war was over was something she never forgot. The cries of happiness and the words to *Song* danced through her memory. It was over, and fear was banished from the lands.

"Why do you tell stories?" Kai asked Triften, kicking her feet in the shallows of the crystal stream, soaking the hem of her skirt. She wore her long, light hair in two braids, the ends trailing almost to her waist.

"Because I must." Triften placed his hands on his knees, leaning forward as an eager blush spread over his face and his words twirled with passion across the waters. "Stories are the key to unlocking truth and looking to our past will inform our future. Just as the original Mermis spread the stories of Heroes of Old, I tell you what I lived through, stories I must pass down in history."

"The war?" a little boy asked, his wet hair standing straight up in the air. He held a hunk of bread in his grubby hands, switching between tossing some to the koi and chewing the rest. "You lived through the war?"

"Aye." Citrine watched Triften's piercing blue eyes grow cloudy in remembrance as he spoke. "The War between the Mortals and Immortals. And now I give you these stories so you will remember what they did to make these realms free in the name of what is good and right. Remember those stories and when your time comes, you will continue the tradition and pass these tales down to your children and grandchildren and great-grandchildren. We cannot forget those who were brave when no one else was, who stepped out of hiding and faced a foe we cannot imagine. The Heroes of Old are the ones who gave you your freedom and allowed you to live in this land without fear."

Triften paused and held up a finger. He was a slim male, only five and a half feet tall. Despite his small stature, he had the ability to command attention. Citrine mused as she listened; perhaps it was his confidence that first drew her attention to him.

"There's another reason I give you the gift of stories. Tales give us empathy and help us see from other points of view. When you listen to a story, you gain a perspective on the world. Perhaps one you've never considered. When you hear a story, you realize anything is possible."

"Tell us the story about the wind lady." Kai interrupted Triften's lecture and clasped her hands together, her eyes shining.

"Ah . . ." Triften smiled. "Look who joined us."

Citrine realized she'd been spotted as Triften's beaming face turned in her direction. He was a Cron—a people group with a light complexion known for their restlessness and love of adventure. Aside from his aura of authority, he had arched eyebrows, full lips, a square jaw, and a long nose. All things considered, he was attractive, but it was his eyes that gave her pause. Considering her past, she had a weakness for eyes. Triften's were deep and soulful, almost as if he'd seen too much and there was nothing left but a calm kindness wavering behind them to observe the coming calamity.

Her innate desire to flirt died in his presence and although she approached him in a coy manner, his mannerisms were surprising. Most males leered at her with malicious intent, thinking of nothing but what was between her legs. Disparaging gestures and inappropriate remarks often followed. Citrine was well aware the way she dressed and walked only encouraged them. It also gave her plenty of opportunity to work out her sharp tongue and get abusive if the situation demanded it. She used to enjoy the pleasures of the flesh until . . .

She let her memories melt away as she walked into the circle of waterfalls.

"Go on with your story," Citrine encouraged Triften, watching the white-and-orange koi brush past her, their whiskers tickling her bare legs. Their mouths opened and closed as they eyed her, but they scattered away when they discovered she held no treats.

"Citrine!" Kai shouted, patting the slick rock she sat on. "Sit with me."

Patting the children on their light heads as she passed, Citrine joined Kai, tucking her legs under her as Triften continued his tale. The children of the village smiled at her, their faces bright with laughter and eyes wide with wonder as Triften weaved a tale. Citrine knew he'd had the great honor of traveling with Eliesmore the Great Conqueror who saved the Four Worlds from the rule of darkness. Triften told a tale of enchantment and horror. He spoke of a great beast who threatened the Torrents Towers—a city of towers in the west—and how the One coaxed the gates to open and rippled the land from the hold of darkness without casualties. He told of the wind in the Monoxie Meadows and how it enchanted a captain of the guards and stole him away from the army.

When his tale was done, the children sat hushed. Citrine felt Kai's fingers creep into hers, squeezing her hand. Straightening her back, Citrine slid a foot back into the cool waters as a wishful sensation crept through her. The desire for a child was not a future dream, yet her friendship with Kai made her wish, sometimes, for a different path in life.

"Citrine." Triften stood and joined her as the children scattered. "Will you walk with me back to the village?"

"Aye," she agreed, the words tumbling out of her mouth before she could stop herself. The fingers of her free hand twitched over her handkerchief, a reminder she needed to gather herbs. She brushed the flicker of worry away as she fell in step with Triften.

"You look concerned." His voice was smooth and tender as he peered at her, curiosity beaming out of his somber eyes.

"Nay, I heard you were back. What brought you here?" Citrine shook off his intrusive question.

His lips turned down and his eyes slithered away, glancing toward the Standing Stones while the children dashed ahead, giggling, making their way back to the village. When Triften was in the land, he gathered the children from each hut and amused them with stories before walking them back to the village around midday.

"Something mysterious?" Citrine teased, reaching out a finger to poke his shoulder.

Triften turned his eyes back to her, one of his lips tugging itself up into a half smile. "I have friends in the west who made a choice I disagree with." He sighed. "I came here because this may be my last chance to talk any sense into them."

"They are coming here?" Citrine glanced around the land, looking for signs of an intruder. She couldn't help but think of all newcomers as intruders, with Triften being the exception.

Triften called the fortress in the southeast home, yet he seemed to roam the lands like a nomad. He gained friends everywhere he went, and traveling across the Jaded Sea to lands of the west did not faze him. Citrine could sense the patience in his calm and intentional steps and the way he paused before he spoke, thinking through his thoughts and concisely responding.

"Aye, at least they told me they would—this being their last stop on their way out."

"Tell me, what did they do? Why don't you agree with them?"

Triften chuckled, his eyes crinkling with laugh lines.

"You will meet them. I'd like you to have an unbiased opinion when you do. Tell me about yourself. How is life in the land? I recall my first visit here—you'd just come through the dark forest."

Citrine frowned, anxious about the request of the night. "My time runs short today. I came to the Standing Stones to gather herbs, but I must be away. Perhaps tonight there will be time. Will you dine at the house of Novor Tur-Woodberry?"

Curiosity danced through Triften's light eyes as he gazed at Citrine, but the words that came out of his mouth were calm and polite. "Perhaps, if he invites me, I will go."

Citrine blinked. "I will be sure he extends an invitation."

Triften turned his body toward her, an odd look coming over his face. "You dine there often?"

"Yes, I am a guest," Citrine blurted out, her defenses rising.

"I meant no harm, only, it is unheard—"

"Don't pretend you know everything about Novor Tur-Woodberry. He has kept these lands for hundreds of years—"

"Ah." Triften lifted a hand, squeezing Citrine's shoulder. "I mean no harm. Until tonight then, my friend. We shall dine at the house of Novor Tur-Woodberry."

Citrine nodded, moving away from Triften and the children to return to the Standing Stones where she could gather herbs in peace.

6

KAI'S SECRET

"Citrine." Kai trotted up to her, waving her arms to push the tall grass aside. "Where are you going?"

Citrine spun around, putting a hand on her head to shield her eyes from the brilliant beams of light. "Kai." She paused. Novor Tur-Woodberry's land was vast, and the village was close to the middle of the land. It would take the better half of the day to walk to the Boundary Line Forest. Unless she called one of her beasts to take her. She toyed with the idea before forgetting it. Her beasts had never entered the sacred land of Novor Tur-Woodberry, and Citrine had never ridden on one. Riding her beasts seemed to desecrate their freedom. She'd never asked.

"I have to meet someone. I have to go," she explained, avoiding Kai's compelling gaze.

Kai snatched up Citrine's hand in her tiny one. "But I

have a secret. I *have* to show you. You're the only one who will understand."

"I will be late," Citrine complained, glancing down at the impetuous child. "Can it wait?"

"Please." Kai tugged on her hand, her light eyes going wide, her lower lip stuck out.

A hint of silver glittered in the child's eyes while Citrine fought with indecision. On one hand, she knew she should head toward the forest before dusk trapped her in the land of Novor Tur-Woodberry. She was unsure how the Master of the Forest handled lateness and she was loath to find out. Discovering Kai's secret was more exciting, and she knew she'd give in, even as the next question left her lips. "Will it take long?"

Kai shook her head, sending her wet braids twisting back and forth on her back. Drops of water sparkled on her eyelashes. "Come with me to the mill." She ran, her fat legs thumping through the grass as she balled up her hands by her side.

Citrine trotted beside her, bare feet digging into the warm soil. A smile came to her cheeks. The wind whipped through her vibrant hair and her heart rate increased as she sped over the rolling hills. A blue bird flew over them, calling out a symphony of melodies, and Citrine let all aggravations fade away in the splendid arms of nature.

The village sat against the swell of lush rolling hills, each one rising higher than the other, creating a myriad vision as they ran toward it. Standing at the top of the Standing Stones, one could see the village covered in a gray mist in the morning and sparkling with light in the daytime. The two lights in the sky, the sun and the Green Light, caused a mystifying glimmer across the land. The inhabitants of Novor Tur-Woodberry's land called it Mouth of Heaven because of the beauty and peace that surrounded it like a beacon of hope.

Thatched-roofed cottages dotted the countryside. They could see sheep and goats grazing in the distance. Brown-spotted cows and pale-pink pigs roamed the hills, rooting and rutting while the fresh scent of herbs rose, faint at first and growing stronger as they neared.

A dirt road, wide enough for a horse and rider, climbed through the center of the Mouth of Heaven, curving to meet the doorstep of each cottage. The people groups worked in the fields, tending to the orchards and their abundant crops, preparing for the coming winter. Citrine was certain they did so with ease, for it seemed nothing went wrong in the blessed land of Novor Tur-Woodberry.

"This way!" Kai shouted, her little legs hidden by the lofty grass. Her arm came up and waved at the mill set in the distance, the windmills slowing down in the lull of the breeze.

A laugh echoed through the air and Citrine spun, her eyes roaming across the prairie.

"What are you doing?" Kai shouted, noticing Citrine was no longer at her side. "Come on!"

"I thought . . ." Citrine cupped her hands around her ears. "I thought I heard a voice in the wind."

"It's because Triften told us the story of the wind lady," Kai teased, her bright eyes squinting as she scrunched up her nose in mischief. "You are thinking of it now and you imagine there is life in the breeze. I think so too. I wish the wind lady would come here and grant all my wishes."

"Kai." Citrine touched the child's shoulder, encouraging her to continue. "The wind lady doesn't grant wishes—at least, I don't remember that from the story."

Kai ran again, her breath coming short and fast as she shouted. "Yes, she does," Her words rushed together in one breath.

"If you had a wish"—Citrine slowed down as they reached a hill and walked up it, trailing their fingers through the long blades of yellow-green grass—"what would you wish for?"

Kai paused, her chest heaving up and down as she wiped wisps of hair from her shiny forehead. "I'd wish to go on an adventure. A real one. Like Triften the Storyteller." Her eyes lit up as the word *adventure* left her tongue. Her eyes sparkled with intense animation as she tilted her head to catch Citrine's gaze. "Don't you want to go on an adventure?"

"Aye," Citrine muttered, unwilling to spoil the child's joy.

Kai grabbed her hand, her soft fingers wrapping

around Citrine's callused ones. "That's why I want to show you the secret," she beamed.

The mill perched before them, a beast humming with a life of its own. The rush of water crashed through the air like the crescendo of an orchestra while crickets chirped in the meadow. A cool breeze floated past, turning the mills on the round white stones. The smell of wheat and grass drifted through the air and a sense of longing gripped Citrine. She squeezed Kai's hand as she headed toward the dark coolness of the building.

"No, not in there." Kai tugged Citrine's arm, leading her to the river that curved through the land, rushing over rocks and stones.

Citrine followed the sparkling river, watching the mist leap off the bank and twirl on the shore. Blue flies buzzed around their heads and the song of the river could almost be deciphered. Every living being and creature in the land seemed to sing, plants and animals alike. A cadence whispered through the air at all times in a song of worship and respect. Deep down inside, she knew what it was: a song for their Healer, Protector, Friend, Guide, and All-Knowing Being. They sang of Novor Tur-Woodberry and his benevolence, generosity, and kindness. Citrine understood the ache deep in her heart, and she longed for a land such as his. A Paradise for her beasts. It was why she wanted to be around him, soaking in his knowledge and asking about his power. How did he create such a haven and how could she create one for her beasts? She hummed under her breath:

"A spell of protection. A spell of disguise.
A spell to hide from prying eyes.
A spell of deflection. A spell of desire.
A spell to hide from seeking eyes."

A stone wall ran across the river. When it narrowed, Kai led Citrine, splashing through water, to the yawning mouth of a cave perched at the base of the hill. "In here." Kai laughed, flinging drops of water off her legs.

Kai held a finger to her lips, eyes sparkling as they entered the cave. Citrine stepped inside, sniffing the wet mud and flavors of water life. Somewhere, a frog croaked and the dragonflies droned on outside, moving away from the damp darkness of the cave. Motes of white light floated past the opening, disappearing into the radiant light of day.

"What is this place?" Citrine lifted her face to the cave ceiling that stretched into blackness, hiding the strength of its size from her.

"I found it playing hide-and-seek with the wood-worker's sons, Aydin and Evyn. But they don't know the secret. If you listen, you can hear it."

Citrine closed her eyes, allowing her ears to take over and listen to the new sensations around her. In the distance, she could hear the wheel of the mill, moving water on down the river so it could grind and crush the wheat into flour. The quacking of ducks fighting over fish burst through the air like ruffled feathers. Closer there was a new sensation. It glided across the hair on her arms, making goosebumps rise on her skin. A deep vibration emitted through the air, like the purr of a multitude of cats basking in satisfaction.

Kai crept through the cave with an air of mystery surrounding her. Her cheeks glowed with pride as she led Citrine around a corner and a light lit up their path.

Citrine's hands flew to her cheeks as she gazed in awe. A white orb hung suspended in midair, touching none of the walls of the cavern, as if it hung from an invisible thread. Bubbles of white light made up the orb, and it pulsed like a heartbeat as the light threaded its way through the cave walls. Citrine gaped in shock at the brilliance and beauty it contained, and a thousand questions flew to her lips. Glancing down at the child, she asked, "Who else knows about this?"

"No one." Kai eyed the ball of energy and put a finger to her lips. "It's our secret. Isn't it amazing?"

"I wonder," Citrine murmured to herself, "if Novor Tur-Woodberry knows about this . . ." She trailed off as she stepped closer, for it seemed the light called to her.

"I call it the Silver-White Heart," Kai went on, the white light of the orb dancing in her eyes as she stared, spellbound.

Citrine listened to the voice calling out to her from within the light. Reaching out a hand, she moved it up to caress the round body of the orb. As her fingers wove across the pattern of light, a profound sensation of peace gripped her, like arms holding her firm. It pulled her toward the source, imbuing her with the sense of warmth, yet there was also something solid immersed within and full of love.

A pulse shot through her veins, encouraging her to stretch her roots like a plant and grow. It was time for her to take her place in the unending cycle of life, death, and rebirth. The power within compelled her to give back to the heart of the land and use her gifts to bring great blessings upon it. Entranced, she let the light draw her in while voices whispered in her ear.

Pictures flashed before her, visions of either things past or things to come. A voice thrummed deep within her, coursing through her veins as it spoke. A voice mixed with doom and hope rose in a singsong voice.

Behold. A future will come when the mortals must flee and run to the caves and canyons to hide from the domain for the immortals. For those without death will rise, and the Creators will have free will to enact their reign of chaos. Even now, changes are taking place in the universe that will have fatal effects for the Four Worlds. It all began with the liberation of the Green Stone instead of its destruction. The release of uncanny power will be the ultimate downfall of the mortals.

The words floated around her head as unreal as the experience. They dropped from her memory, forgotten as soon as they appeared. Yet the Silver-White Heart pulsed with need, a strong desire, and the power of Novor Tur-Woodberry protected it. Yet as Citrine drew farther in, she saw the tiniest blemish among the purity of the light. A drop of blackness pierced the middle of the heart, like a bad seed in a perfect fruit. A strange feeling of fate came over Citrine and she pulled back, reaching out for Kai.

"Kai." Her voice sounded old and far away when she spoke. "I don't know what this is, but I have to go."

Kai said nothing, only reached out a hand, stroking Citrine's arm for a moment before clasping her hands in front of her and staring into the silver light.

Citrine turned from the enchanting place, her feet unwilling to leave, yet knowing she would be late to the meeting in the Boundary Line Forest. As she fled into the sunshine, the memory of doom echoed in her mind.

7

DARK AND COLD

A POUNDING HEADACHE WOKE TOR LIR. HE turned over and retched into the ground. He opened his eyes as best as he could, the stream of filth pouring from his mouth. He realized, with some grim relief, he was still alive. When the last of the bile left his quaking stomach, he stood to see where he was, wiping his mouth with the back of his hand and rubbing the rest on his jerkin.

Great pine trees rose above him, thick and old as if they had countless stories to tell—only they were asleep. He could almost see their spirits with his naked eyes, long faces with old bodies and dark moss from age, their eyes closed with sleep, for it was too late for them. He turned without making a sound, for his days in the forest of Shimla had taught him to move with stealth. As he eyed his surroundings, he saw a wall of trees rising on all sides with a carpet of pine needles beneath his feet. There was no sign of the beast who had chased and wounded him.

He lifted a hand to his forehead and came away with muddied dry blood. His cuts had closed, although his ankle gave off an old sensation of pain. He hobbled on it, but it was nothing too intense so he decided he could travel on with it. Yet as he glanced around, he could not decide which way to go. The forest closed in on all sides and there was no signal or signs that pointed where to go. Although he wondered, where did he hope to arrive? The sensation of danger that had dragged him from the safety of home in Shimla had faded, leaving him with a vague suspicion that something was wrong. Since leaving the forest, he traveled south, hoping he might discover what was next for him, while the ominous word, *Daygone*, rang in his mind.

Shaking it off, he took a step in a random direction and a flash of white caught his vision. He froze, looking around the forest floor for a kind of weapon. Suddenly, he felt unprepared and naïve in the realm of mortals. He wished he'd studied the ways of the mortals and understood their weapons before he left. He needed help now, and a fear sunk into him, a feeling he had not known for a while. He knew he was immortal, yet it did not mean he was impervious to death. It seemed too soon to die, for his life had just begun and he knew, with certainty, his days held a great purpose. He needed to stay alive.

The flash of white appeared again and, as noisily as a panther stalking its prey, a bone creature appeared beside a pine tree, staring at him. It was a spirit—he could tell that much from his days among the Iaens— and suddenly he wished he knew more lore of the world. Knowledge was lacking among the Iaens. The green giantess who had raised him made it clear: if he wished to know the depths of knowledge, he'd have to search for it. A curiosity awoke within him as he examined the creature.

It was a female made of cold white bone. Her limbs were skeletal and slender. Silver hair, as thin as the gossamer of a spider's web, trailed down her back. Her face looked as if someone carved it out of ivory with deep-set eyes, thin lips, and a chiseled nose that stuck out far too much.

She stared at him out of somber eyes, the color so rich he could not tell whether they were black or brown. Her cheeks were shallow, but he could see a flicker of pain in the sharp features of her wasted face. She took a step toward him, wearing nothing but moss that seemed to grow and twine around her bone body, holding on to the last lingering taste of life.

"Oh," she whispered, her voice high and breathy as if she were trying to keep from crying out in distress.

As she moved toward him, he sensed her aura and saw shades of it flicker around her like a cloak. She did not come to harm him.

"Where am I? Who are you?" he asked, tilting his head, trying to ignore the eerie bone whiteness of her body.

She stared at him, blinking as she moved closer. "You are in the realm of the Master now. Who I am is inconsequential."

Chewing his sore lip, he tried a different method. "Who is the Master? Why am I here?"

"You know why you are here." Her eyes moved to his feet as if she searched for an anchor to reality.

Understanding her meaning, Tor Lir plunged on, hoping at some point he would ask the right question to unlock the answers he sought. "On some level, yes, a beast chased me here, but I suspect for some bigger reason."

"So you will not interfere with the Master's wishes, but I sense you are strong." The creature glanced at his face ever so quickly before dropping her gaze once again.

Tor Lir shrugged. He did not feel very strong, especially after being beaten by the beast. "I'm sorry, but your answers are vague. Will you speak plainly?"

"I may not say." The creature lifted her face and a flash of anger rippled over her eyes.

"Can you tell me which way to go?" Tor Lir huffed with minor impatience.

"It depends on where you want to arrive."

"I would like to seek the Master." He scratched his head, wondering what he was getting himself into.

"He does not want to see you."

"How do you know?" Tor Lir stepped toward her, showing his aggression.

"I do his biding. I know his wishes." The creature

fixed him with a look he could not decipher, although her aura vibrated and a keen fear pierced the air.

"I wonder," he murmured. "Why do you obey the wishes of the Master?"

She gave no answer, only watched him until he spoke again.

"I would like to leave this place."

"Then leave. There is no one stopping you."

"We are talking in circles. This is my first time in the realm of mortals. I am not sure where to go," he admitted.

"Once you discover what you seek, you will know where to go." Bending her head, the bone creature took a step back, displacing the pine needles around her feet.

"Are you a spirit then? You speak with a tact and wisdom beyond your years."

Startled, the creature stared at him, although her face hid her surprise. "I used to be once, before they extorted me. I may not speak of this."

"What *can* you speak of?" Tor Lir asked, his curiosity piquing around the mysterious circumstances. "What was the beast that attacked me? What forest am I in? How will I know what to seek? What is your name?"

The creature tilted her head down and to the side, a white finger coming up to stroke her chin as if considering what risk she would take.

Suddenly, she reached out, her cold fingers locking around his wrist as her face contorted. "Never tell a name," she hissed. "To give a name is to give power. I've already made that mistake and paid dearly for it." Just as quickly, the hostility in her face faded away and letting go of him, she placed a finger to her lips. "Stay here. I must complete a task for the Master. When I return, I will lead you out of this restless maze."

A shudder passed through Tor Lir as her touch vanished from his arm. He watched as she backed away and off in the distance, he thought he heard a piercing cry. Anxiety settled deep in his bones and a strong premonition gripped him. The balance was off, swinging the wrong way, and he needed to fix it.

8

HOME

Novor Tur-Woodberry lifted the jug of sparkling liquid and refilled his mug, watching the bubbles pop as they fizzled in the bottom of his cup. Around him the Fúlishités pulled their chairs up in a circle, the roaring fire crackling in the background although it was summer. The warm circle of the hut was often cool in the evenings and the fire provided warmth as they eased their muscles from a glorious day spent tramping through the land. Some lit pipes of tobacco, the musky flavors floating through the air, while others poured their mugs full of ale or wine, relishing in the fruit of the labor of their hands. A somber air rested over the home—not one of fear, only of the understanding of a challenge.

Novor Tur-Woodberry took a long sip, watering his throat before he spoke. "A change is coming over the land, a problem we haven't had before," he told his Singing Men.

They nodded, their eyes sharp and intelligent, although they often hid their words behind songs of praise and lore.

"This morning, I was made aware of a darkness creeping into the land. As far as I know, it began in the marshes and has not spread farther. I inspected the borders but need your assistance with it. If there is anything or anyone out of the ordinary, they must be brought to our attention. We will deal with them as we do best. There is something new in the land, a favorable presence, but it has not made itself known. I will look into it tomorrow. Are there any other reports?"

"The Storyteller returned." Ash, one of the Singing Men, blew a cloud of smoke out of his mouth as he spoke. His eyes were black like berries and sharp as they shifted back and forth. He was stout with thick muscles on his arms and legs. Wiry brown hair—which was thinning—stuck out of his head and he often scratched it.

"Ah, he is harmless enough," Teak, another one of the Singing Men, chimed in. "Although methinks he has an agenda, showing up here so often."

"Aye, he should move into the village with the others." Balsa nodded into his mug of ale. His eyelashes were long and light while his face had somewhat of a sleepy look to it.

"Inhabitants of the land are free to come and go as they please," Novor Tur-Woodberry remarked. "It's not his presence I mention but one of another species, a sort of spirit. Tomorrow, I must go seek the wisdom of the land, with the sudden darkness I am curious about the fulfillment of an old prophecy."

"What prophecy?" snapped Jatoba. He bristled on the outside, yet he was one of the more softhearted Singing Men. His hair was a copper color, and he kept his beard in two braids that almost reached his waist. "I thought we were done with prophets and visions after the rise of the One . . ." He trailed off, muttering into his ale.

"Nothing is certain in life." Novor Tur-Woodberry grunted. "The land has rested well after the Great Conqueror, but there is always mischief and mayhem that follows. It is our job to rise to the challenge and not let it defeat our spirits. Nothing is certain yet, but we must prepare for what comes. Let us eat and drink and discuss as we do and make no certain claims until we have more information on the morrow. I sense something is happening in the world that will affect us all—what it is, I can't be sure—but something went wrong during the days of the war between the mortals and immortals. Something went wrong, and we will reap the repercussions of that mistake."

"Every action invokes another action." Ash nodded his wise head. "Do you think it has anything to do with Citrine? She is hiding something."

Novor Tur-Woodberry chuckled. Citrine was spunky and full of spirit, yet he doubted if the changes of his land were due to her presence. "She is not powerful enough." He shook his head, glancing into his mug. "Unless I've missed something."

"And you miss nothing," Ash said.

"Aye, what's that?" Jatoba spoke up again as a banging sounded at the door.

"It's Triften," the person on the other side of the door called out.

"Who invited him?" Jatoba frowned.

"Oh ho, that's not how we treat guests in this land," Novor Tur-Woodberry boomed. "Let him in," he addressed the house.

Triften the Storyteller strode into the house and stopped short, his eyes examining the gathering around the fire. His arms and legs were so long and limber he often appeared taller than he truly was. His blue eyes widened and his shoulders relaxed with relief.

Novor Tur-Woodberry held out a hand toward a chair. "Come. Seat yourself."

About twenty or so years ago, Triften made his first appearance in the land. He was quite young, still in his teen years and had an air of devotion about him. Everything inspired him with awe until the incident. Something took place over ten years ago, and Triften came limping back to the land, his innocence replaced with the bitter tang of loss. Sorrow inspired him to find a purpose, and he grew into a confident leader with one goal: to seek knowledge.

"Citrine isn't here?" Triften's eyes danced across the

room and then he sat down, a slight smile coming to his lips.

"Nay, have a drink." Novor Tur-Woodberry waved a tankard of ale over to Triften. It moved on its own accord, perching on the arm of the chair Triften sat in.

Triften shrugged. "When we spoke earlier, she mentioned dining here tonight."

"Are you concerned?"

"To be honest, aye. Her actions bother me. Have you noticed anything peculiar since she appeared here?"

Novor Tur-Woodberry put down his drink and reached for his pipe, tapping tobacco into it. The speculations coming out of Triften's mouth were not surprising, but Novor Tur-Woodberry sensed Triften had a unique motive for bringing it up. Declining to play games, he turned the conversation back on Triften. "What concerns you about her?"

"Her motives. She did not come to the land to dwell in harmony with others. I sense something is stirring and there is a darkness at the edges of the land. She works with herbs and runes. I can't help but assume it is her doing, but this is your land. I do not want to overstep my welcome here."

Novor Tur-Woodberry hummed as he inhaled. The smoke from his pipe billowed in his mouth and wisps of peace snaked through his body. An uncanny brightness followed Citrine, but she did not have the ability to inflict change on his land. Sitting back in his chair, he closed his eyes, listening to the flicker of the fire and allowing himself to sink into the river of knowledge he'd gathered from his years in the South World.

He held a distinct awareness of the comings and goings of every living creature on his land, and at the moment, he could tell Citrine was not there. She'd gone somewhere earlier that evening, east, to the Boundary Line Forest. When he first met her, she was limping and dirty, as if she'd wrangled with those in the forest. He gathered there was something there she cared about, yet she did not offer to come clean about her past dealings.

Novor Tur-Woodberry pursed his lips into an O and blew out a cloud of smoke. It hung above his head in a white haze. Perhaps there was something he'd overlooked and Citrine held answers. Considering the darkness creeping over his borders, he needed to speak with her soon. He'd send the Singing Men to ensure she came to dinner and could relate her tale. She harbored a weakness for him. That much was clear in her strange eyes and the way her lips smiled at him.

"I will speak with her," Novor Tur-Woodberry said. "What else lies heavy on your mind?"

"The wind lady comes with a gift. I don't agree with her intentions, but your knowledge is greater than mine. She decided her time here is done, and she is leaving to seek the Beyond, but she has children. I don't understand why she desires to leave them."

Triften's parents abandoned him during the days of war—it was a scar Novor Tur-Woodberry knew he'd never healed from. Peace in the land allowed families to dwell together without fear of being ripped apart by evil. Someone might see Triften's intentions as interfering with others' freedoms.

"Your thoughts are respected, but I remind you, it is not my purpose to interfere with others' choices, unless they impact the safety of my lands and its inhabitants."

Triften nodded and took a long sip of ale, gulping down the liquid as if it would give him strength. His lips were moist when he sat the tankard down. His blue eyes glistened as he moved to the edge of his seat. "Have you heard whispers about the new breed?"

Visions of peace evaporated and Novor Tur-Woodberry took the pipe from his mouth, frowning at the unexpected question. "The new breed? What do you speak of?" he demanded, although he knew, repetition seeped through history and something was overlooked during the war. "Tell me, why do you speak of a new breed?"

Triften's eyes glinted with curiosity. "I was hoping you might tell me."

9

REALM OF NIGHT

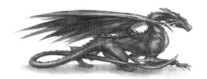

"AVA," CITRINE WHISPERED, SKIPPING BETWEEN the beams of silver light as she entered the Boundary Line Forest. Afraid of being late to the unwanted meeting, she'd asked one of the wild horses of Novor Tur-Woodberry's land to give her a ride to the forest. The white steed was delighted with adventure, and if Citrine's thoughts hadn't been churning with a dark foreboding, she would have enjoyed the fierce gallop through Paradise.

As she slipped into the wood, she noted a distinct shift in the air, the pure beauty of Paradise marred by the dense secrets of the gloomy forest. It seemed as if evil fingers reached out to squeeze her heart. Citrine shivered, but not with fear. Her first journey through the Boundary Line Forest had been unforgiving, a mix of adventure and terror playing mischievous games as they chased her out. All she had was hope that things would be different. "Ava," she whispered again, strands of moonbeams swaying around her like knives.

A rustling in the leaves drew her attention and hurling out of the darkness, scales flashing in the light, appeared a beast. Her fierce head looked like a wyvern with a long snout and a row of curved sharp teeth. A puff of smoke drifted from her nostrils, quickly dissipating into the night. Her lengthy neck was thick, much like a sea eel, while the rest of her body moved on four clawed legs, stout like the monsters of the night. A hard coat of scales and feathers covered her blue and green body.

Citrine. A voice resounded within Citrine's mind.

Ava. You're beautiful. Look how you've grown.

Reaching up, she placed her palm on Ava's snout. Ava arched her neck, bringing it down to rest on Citrine's shoulder, a purr-like hum rumbling through her body.

Have you come to take us away? Ava asked.

Citrine bit her lip. *Perhaps . . . I came because I missed you and . . . there is a request. Have you spoken to Morag?*

We see him from time to time. Ava's golden eyes shifted. *Methinks he is associated in some nasty business with the Master of the Forest.*

Is that so? Can you follow and confirm for me? I don't like being summoned here as if I were a mouthpiece without my own mind.

I can kill him for you. Ava hissed, her forked tongue flicking in and out as her odd eyes glowed.

Citrine grinned, the idea of mischief stirring within her like a spark. *That's the spirit, but no. We need Morag— he's one of us, new as he is. And I am curious to know what the Master of the Forest wants. Observe and report. We'll meet again here, one week from now under the moonlight. As usual. Where are Zaul and Grift? Have you been with them?*

Ava tossed her head, withdrawing to the darkness. *Grift went south. There is a village beyond the forest, close to the shore, with, perhaps, the best fish in the world. You know how Grift likes fish. He claims he can see the story of the waves when he bites into the flesh of a sea creature.*

Citrine rolled her eyes. *Grift is always thinking up strange ways to gain knowledge. A simple conversation would suffice instead of biting into anything to see if it has a story.*

You asked. Ava retreated farther, her eyes gleaming.

Where are you going? Citrine ignored the beast's sarcastic response. Ava was impatient and impulsive, and if restricted, she complained.

You gave me a mission. I must go find Morag.

Citrine watched the glowing eyes fade into the trees and the monstrous form of Ava disappear from view. Her beasts were odd. They came to her from dark and shadow, binding themselves to her and her wishes, because their eyes were the same color. Citrine. They were dangerous, yet she had a strong desire to protect them. She'd failed before and needed the spell so she would not fail them again.

Ava. Be careful.

There is nothing but risk in all we do. The link to Ava

faded like seeds disappearing into soil. There. But unseen.

Citrine put her hands on her hips, tapping her foot as she waited in the glade. She turned around and gasped at the creature that appeared from behind a tree trunk. The creature was lithe with silver hair as if she stepped from a moonbeam. Her brittle bones were thin and her eyes high and sunken. Her skin was pale, and she held out a skull before her in both hands like a present. "Are you the one they call Citrine?" the waif asked, her voice high and thin.

Citrine looked the creature up and down, a strong feeling of unease settling in her bones. "Aye." She gave a sharp nod, hesitant to speak to the creature. "And who might you be?"

"I am supposed to give you this." The creature glanced down at the skull. "To bury in the middle of the land they call Paradise."

Citrine snorted. "Why? You can't expect me to go bury a skull in the land of Novor Tur-Woodberry!"

The waif dropped her eyes. "It is not I who does the asking . . ."

Citrine paused, understanding dawning. "Ah, you are the messenger from the Master of the Forest." She dropped her eyes to the skull to examine it. At first, she'd assumed it was the skull of a mortal like herself; however, it seemed to be the skull of a beast with a misshapen head and a long snout. The sockets for eyes were wide and round like antlers or horns sawn to the nub. A deep foreboding gripped Citrine's belly, and she stepped back, suddenly feeling lightheaded. She shook her head at the shining creature. "No. I refuse. I'm not taking that foul skull to Paradise."

The creature took a step closer to Citrine, her white form glowing in the moonlight like the undead. Her face appeared wasted, but her eyes glowed with an arcane luster as she pressed the skull into Citrine's stomach. "You can—you don't have a choice. Your beasts will die in this forest unless you follow the wishes of the Master."

"Are you threatening me?" Citrine demanded, her fingers wrapping around the cold skull despite herself. "I will call my beasts and leave—"

The waif held up a hand, hushing Citrine, her eyes burning brighter. "You called your beasts, and did they come? One did, but the others scattered because of the Master. Now go, bury the skull before you must bury one of your beasts."

A wail of fury rose within Citrine and her face turned hot and red. She glowered at the creature, her fingers tightening around the skull, willing it to break and shatter.

"The skull is resilient. You cannot break it." The waif glared at Citrine and the light went out of her eyes.

Citrine stepped back a few paces, a chill coming over her like a shadow of death. Her heartbeat increased as liquid pooled around her body, rising to her neck as if she'd fallen into a lake. A hand gripped her head, pushing her down into the liquid until it poured into her mouth, invading her lungs. She opened her mouth to breathe and nothing but fire poured down her throat, eating her innards alive. Voices whispered through her head, the malicious meaning made clear. *Do as I tell you, or your beasts will suffer. Just like the creatures of flesh.*

Her eyes flew open as the odd simulation left her and she took deep breaths, turning her back to the waif so it wouldn't see her fear.

"Citrine." The creature grabbed her wrist with fingers like frost. The strange glow in her eyes faded. She appeared pale, lost, and tired. "Beware. The Master of the Forest is cruel and powerful. He is coming for Paradise because the balance has swayed and none can stand before him. Do not underestimate him."

BONE-WHITE

TOR LIR SLUMPED AGAINST THE BASE OF A TREE, listening to the occasional silence of the wood. The wind rushed through the treetops while animals rustled through the deep thickets. A malicious intent hung in the air, a sharp reminder of impending danger and how different this forest was from the forest of the Iaens.

He waited patiently, calming his mind with the practice of unconsciousness. It was something he'd learned from the Iaens. After discovering he did not need to sleep like mortals, he still liked to maintain a sense of rest by stilling his mind and turning off his churning thoughts. The concentration was something like meditation, allowing him to empty his mind and focus his energy on something specific.

There in the forest he focused on healing his body, his mind sensing each limb, searching for the brokenness and fixing it. The blood under his bruises spread out, new blood filtering through his veins. The cuts on his face closed with new skin forming over them. He stretched his ankle, letting the bruises heal while the knots in his stomach faded, leaving a vague sensation of hunger and thirst. He brushed those aside, hoping his needs would be met soon. For now, he had to wait.

"You're still here." The bone-white creature crept toward him.

Tor Lir started and stood, resting a hand on the rough trunk of a pine tree. "I waited, as you instructed," he told her, noticing her aura. A heaviness surrounded her, and she felt both sorry and guilty about something.

"Where were you?" he dared to ask.

"Nowhere that concerns you." Her voice melted into the silence of the night, her head downcast as she moved beside him. "Follow me."

She led him through the trees, moving with a surprising quickness as he strode silently behind. She glanced back now and then with an anxious look in her eye, checking to ensure he really was behind her.

They moved like those in a dream, while the beasts of the night hunted and fought, departing from the realm of hunter and hunted on to safer passages. Blackness hung over the forest like a blanket of death, and a rottenness hung in the air, making it dense and musty.

Finally, they came to a place where the trees thinned, and it surprised Tor Lir to look up and see the moonlight hanging in the night sky like a silver slice of light. He paused, waiting for the bone-white creature to speak.

When at last she turned to face him, liquid filled her dark eyes.

"Go now, back to whence you came," she cautioned him. "The less you know, the better."

He reached out a hand, a wave of compassion coming over him for the beautiful, lost spirit. "You still have empathy—you still have a heart," he told her, although he did not know her. Something inside him called to her. There was a reason he'd met her in the frightful wood. "I can help you, if you will let me."

She bowed her head. "You are kind, yet you know nothing. Go back. Go home. Forget this wild day and what you saw and heard here. Your very life depends upon it."

He reached out a hand, cupping her thin cheek, whispering words into her ear. "Why did you help me? Perhaps there is a way I can repay your kindness."

"It was not kindness," she said, a sharpness returning to her eyes. She pulled away from his touch, shuddering. "It was mercy."

BURIED SKULL

THE SCREAM OF PANIC DIED IN CITRINE'S throat when she took in her surroundings. The wide-eyed fear faded from her eyes and her heartbeat slowed. Gentle sunlight filled her eyes, and the breeze blew over her face. She patted the ground with her fingers as she took in her location. It appeared she'd slept in the heart of the land of Novor Tur-Woodberry. She stood up, her bones aching in discomfort as she brushed dried mud off her hand. *What happened?* The question flittered through her mind. The sky was blue and empty while the whispers of joy hushed through the land. *What did I do?*

Citrine. The connection to one of her beasts filtered into her consciousness.

Grift! Where are you?

You seem panicked and worried. Is it happening again?

I think so. I can't remember everything that happened last night. After the waif and the skull, my memory is hazy. But I know the Master of the Forest is coming for Paradise. We have to run!

Citrine.

You don't agree?

You know I will always do what you ask, but we can't always run. The world will box us into a corner, and there will be no other choice but to stand and fight.

Is that wisdom you learned from the fish?

Sea creatures travel far and wide. They know many things and were kind to sacrifice their lives to share their wisdom with me.

Grift.

You may not agree, but it is truth. Knowledge is the key to unlocking desires. Once you know the secrets of one's heart, you can gain anything and everything you desire. Knowledge will make you invincible.

What are you suggesting?

I suggest you face this challenge head-on.

Grift.

I know you have reservations, but we can't always run. At least, not from the chaos we create. We must make things right.

We did not start this.

Perhaps. But we caused it. I know not what you learned when you spoke with the Master of the Forest—

No, that thing, that creature has a strong desire, and I made a promise I cannot break without risking the life of you and me.

Don't forget who you are.

Citrine fell silent, the words stinging like a slap in the face. *Do you think I deserve to be happy again?*

I think you deserve what you want to deserve.

Chewing her lip, she studied the intricate pattern the grass weaved, a circle within a circle, spiraling out in four directions: north, south, east, and west. A star seemed to twinkle within the circle, yet as she studied the pattern, she became sure it was just an illusion. The command to bury the skull came drifting back, and she squinted before kneeling in the grass. Running her fingers through the thick blades, she tried to find the place where she had ripped through the dirt, tearing it to pieces so she could bury the skull. There was no sign of digging. The grass rippled over the knoll without ceasing.

Placing her hands on her knees, she tapped her fingers as scenarios ran through her thoughts. Unpleasant memories rose in her mind, a blur of visions and smells. There was a reason she'd been driven away from her past life—a mixture of truth, lies, and secrets had ruined her potential. Her assumed journey of life took a nasty turn. She rose to her feet, her brow furrowed with concern.

Grift.

You have a request?

Only a question. Have you seen Zaul recently?

Nay, are you concerned?

Slightly. I've heard from you and Ava but not Zaul. I might have to find him.

I can look—

No! Do not risk your safety and freedom. I want you with

me, here in Paradise. I asked Ava to do something dangerous for me and now I am concerned about her. Don't look—just come to the land.

Ah . . . you want to face this challenge head-on?

Yes, I will face this challenge, but first, I must speak to Novor Tur-Woodberry. He owns these lands and he should know who I am and what I have brought here.

You care about what he thinks.

Citrine crossed her arms, pulling a face at Grift's remark. *I am a guest in his land. Of course I care what he thinks,* she retorted.

The connection to Grift faded, an empty roar as Citrine lifted her face to the sunlight. Ever since she'd stepped foot in the land, a deep love for nature coursed through her veins. She doubted she could handle it if anything happened to the Paradise she'd discovered. For a moment, she wondered if she should return to her cottage to freshen up before hastening to the house of Novor Tur-Woodberry. She bit her tongue in contemplation as she eyed the sun. Novor Tur-Woodberry was sure to be out surveying his land. He seemed to work tirelessly yet could always be found at home when evening fell. If she took the day, she still had time to gather herbs and complete the spell.

"Citrine," a familiar voice called, an unspoken question ringing out.

Citrine spun like someone caught stealing, her face turning bright red. She hid her hands behind her back, hoping he wouldn't notice the dirt on them, the wrinkles on her dress, or the way her hair hung wild and uncombed. Out of the corner of her eye, she saw the leaves of a dandelion tangled in threads of her hair. She snatched at it as she spoke. "Triften?"

"Aye, I am surprised to find you here. Although, I must admit, I'm not sure of your daily habits. I went to the house of Novor Tur-Woodberry last night, but you weren't there."

"Ah." Citrine kept her expression blank as she met his eyes. "Something came up."

"Oh." His eyes traveled over her body, taking in her shoddy appearance. "Is something wrong?" His eyes creased with worry.

"Nothing at all," Citrine snapped. "I lost track of time and must hurry on now. Perhaps I'll see you tonight." Turning her back to him, she ran in the opposite direction, away from the questioning words, too quickly to see the look of complete and utter befuddlement come over Triften's face.

WIND LADY

NOVOR TUR-WOODBERRY STOOD IN THE GROVE, watching the breeze frolic through the heavily adorned branches. A mischievous laugh sprinkled through the green leaves and white blossoms while the woodland animals came out of their homes to watch the show.

"Visitors," whispered a chipmunk to a shrew rat. "The visitors are here."

"Where?" a wet-nosed weasel asked a bright-eyed hedgehog. "I see nothing unusual at all."

"It's in the trees," a bright-eyed bird told a grasshopper, and then, realizing the grasshopper was a dumb beast, ate it whole.

The wind whistled through the age-old oak trees as if it were the beginnings of a cyclone. Novor Tur-Woodberry alone stood unmoved as the winds rushed over him. His baritone voice lifted in laughter as he called out, "Welcome, visitor to my land. Don't be bashful—show yourself!"

A sharp snap rang through the grove as if someone broke a thousand tree branches at once. The wind circled Novor Tur-Woodberry, who planted his feet and crossed his muscular arms over his broad chest. "Oh ho, why resist? We are all friends here."

"Friends?" The cyclone whirled, turning into a solid mass and revealing the newcomer to the land. Wild hair trailed around her shoulders, bouncing up again as if coasting on an invisible breeze. Her arms were bare and brown and her eyes were bright and inquisitive. She glanced around the grove, noting the creatures who scurried in attendance, noses quivering as they observed her. Placing a hand on her hip, she smiled, her voice low and sensuous as she spoke. "Legend tells of your land, Novor Tur-Woodberry." She dipped her head as if bowing to a higher being. "Long have I desired to come here and bring you a gift—the only thing missing in your land."

"A gift is quite generous of you." Novor Tur-Woodberry chuckled. "I sense a deeper discussion must take place. Come along and dine at my home."

The lady held up a hand, her eyes narrowing as she shook her head, a laugh spilling from her lips. "Is that your way? Invite all guests to dine at your home? A magical realm I suppose where you pull thoughts and ideas from the heads of your guests and spin them into tales of your own creation? Just because legend speaks of you does not mean I am ready to enter your home. First, I wish to walk your land, to ensure it is as great and as good as legend tells. Only then will I reveal my gift."

"Ah." Novor Tur-Woodberry's eyes twinkled. "You come with a challenge, yet I felt your presence in the land yesterday. What have you learned since you arrived?"

"Many things, but not enough. All I have seen lies on the surface. I must go beyond what is seen and understand the deeper mysteries of your land."

"Some mysteries are not meant to be discovered," Novor Tur-Woodberry said. "But come, I will show you the land myself. Walk through it. Speak with the inhabitants. Everything lives and breathes with life here, kept with my powers. The secrets you wish to find shall be revealed to you, while others will remain locked away. There should always be a limit to knowledge."

The lady smiled. "Perhaps. You will always speak your version of the truth, but you are not the only one powerful enough to control this land."

"Ah, you speak of things which should be discussed with a pint of ale and a pipe of tobacco. This conversation would be welcomed around my table."

The lady raised a hand, brushing his words aside. "No doubt, but you forget. Your land is missing someone vital, and you haven't realized your great need. The greatest Duneíthaír in all the land had something else."

"You speak of the power of life and death—a power known to only the greatest Healer of the past?"

"Ah, so you know the tales."

"You doubt my knowledge. I know that you are the wind lady and my guess is that you have come to grace my land with the gift of wind. One of your twin daughters?"

She smiled then, showing off a row of perfectly white teeth. Wind seemed to rush around her, caressing her hair and tugging at her sky-blue dress. For a moment, she blended into the grove, almost invisible with the sky and land.

"I am the wind lady, come from worlds apart. I come because my days are numbered. My winds are blowing eastward and an impossible call is pulling me onward, yet my heart belongs here in this land." She cast her face to the side, eyes down as a pensive look came over her. "I will inspect your land before I reveal why I need your help."

Compassion covered Novor Tur-Woodberry's face, and he nodded. His tone was gentle as he spoke. "I hear you and I encourage you. Go through my lands, speak to those who live there, and let your mind rest at ease. There is nothing but welcome here for you."

Although she appeared cryptic, Novor Tur-Woodberry knew her story. She'd captured the heart of a captain and spirited him away in the Monoxie Meadows. They lived happily for a time, giving birth to two daughters. Novor Tur-Woodberry guessed the wind lady left one of her daughters to roam the Monoxie Meadows while the other she hoped to leave in his land. From there, she and Captain Elidar would begin their final journey to the Pillars of Creation.

The moment shattered and a voice shouted, "Novor Tur-Woodberry! Novor Tur-Woodberry! We need your help!"

LAVENDER AND LEMON

CITRINE FLUNG OPEN THE DOOR TO HER cottage and slammed it shut, leaning against it as she caught her breath. Shaking her hair out of her face, she stumbled into the dark, making her way to the fireplace where day-old ash had gathered. During the night, the wind had thrust its way down her chimney, scattering soot and ash across the cool stone floor like a thief searching for treasure. High windows let in glimpses of daylight, making patterns in the floor. As much as Citrine loved the sunlight, sometimes she preferred to work in dim light.

Striking flint against a stone, she caught a flame and laid it on the fireplace among the charred wood from yesterday. Reaching for her basket and some additional sticks, she drew up short when she discovered her basket of herbs was not hanging by the fireplace. She tossed the sticks in hand into the fire, letting it sputter and flicker to life. She huffed, peering through the darkness to find her basket. "I had it yesterday," she swore, running back through her memories and coming up with nothing. The strange waif who had given her the skull seemed to have taken her memories.

Stumbling to her worktable, Citrine riffled through herbs scattered there, an increasing sense of discomfort coming over her. It seemed someone had searched her cottage. Nothing was in its place. The herbs, parchment, rock, and candle were gone.

Soot smudged her fingers and when she tried to brush them off on her clothes, she turned them black. It was a moment before she noticed someone was pounding on the door.

Snatching up a lemon rind, she sucked on it as she made her way to the door, her mind distracted with the ingredients of the memory tea she needed to make. Flinging open the door, she peered down at the four-foot-tall creature who stood before it. It was one of Novor Tur-Woodberry's Singing Men. If she recalled correctly, his name was Teak.

His cheeks turned rosy at the sight of her disorderly appearance. "Milady Citrine." He almost gave a mock bow but paused before dipping his head, grinning rather rudely at her. "Seems I've interrupted you. Nevertheless, I was asked to check on you. You were missing at dinner last night and apparently you were expected."

"Apparently." Citrine bit her lip. Novor Tur-Woodberry had never sent someone to check on her before. "Well, as you can see, I'm fine."

She slammed the door on his imprudence, glancing down at her wrinkled and now torn dress. She'd have to change. Her belly rumbled with hunger as she made her way through her disorderly cottage. The fire smoked into the room while she searched for the kettle to prop up on top. Her heart beat with a fury at the idea someone had entered her home and riffled through her personal effects.

She spit out her lemon rind at the sound of a thump on her door. Tossing it into the fire, she made her way back to the door, yelling, "I said I was fine. Leave me alone!"

She jerked open the door to Teak's judging face. This time, she noticed a few of the other Singing Men in the distance waiting. "Errr . . . yes, I know." He scratched his head sheepishly as if embarrassed to ask. "You are invited to dinner tonight at the house of Novor Tur-Woodberry. Will you attend?"

Citrine frowned. "I might be busy," she admitted, although she was reluctant to miss an evening. As much as she wanted to speak with Novor Tur-Woodberry, she needed to figure out her situation, which was unraveling. "I have a question." She narrowed her eyes at Teak, who had backed away.

"Eh?"

"Have you or Novor Tur-Woodberry or any of the

Singing Men ever had a wife?" She spit out the words, her ears burning with the daring question.

Confusion crept into Teak's eyes. "What do you speak of? We run the land. There is no time."

"But you eat, drink, and relax every night," Citrine insisted, unsure why she pressed the embarrassing question. "Undoubtedly, there have been visitors that caught your eye."

"Perhaps there have been. We have lived many years, but all stories are told at the house of Novor Tur-Woodberry. You know this. So come tonight if you want to know more." Teak stepped back, gave a jolly laugh, and turned to join the Singing Men. With a shout, they were off, marching through the land without a care in the world. As they faded from view, Citrine heard a song drift over the rolling hills, voices lifted in praise and admiration of the greatness of Novor Tur-Woodberry.

"Useless Singing Men," she muttered. "If I had people sing about my greatness all day, I'd do something more with my life." A hot surge of jealousy whizzed through her as she slammed the door, returning to search for her missing herbs.

A sprig of lavender appeared, and she lifted it, cradling the leaves as the teakettle boiled. Search as she might, she could not find any more lavender. With a sigh, she tossed her wrinkled clothes on the floor and poured herself a cup of tea. Brushing ash off the hearth, she sat cross-legged in front of the fire. She placed lavender leaves in the cup and hunched over it, breathing in. She needed to relax and clear her mind before she hunted for more herbs. She needed ginseng to bring back the memories of last night, plus the ingredients for her spell of protection were gone. She had to start over.

Drawing her knees up to her chest, she wrapped her arms around them and rocked back and forth as the scent of lavender seeped into her skin. Waves of panic floated around her, and she reached down a finger, drawing patterns in the debris from the fireplace.

Her past life flashed before her. Chocolate-brown eyes. Tender kisses. Laughing in the light until she thought her heart would explode from happiness. The herb garden and her beasts, secrets, lies, and joy wrapped together in one bundle until everything exploded. Impatiently, she brushed the angry thoughts away, destroying the rune she'd written in the ash. She needed to focus if this would work. Why couldn't she remember? What if she had done something evil? Was the Master of the Forest coming for her? She'd kept up her end of the bargain . . .

A knock came at the door, breaking her concentration. Citrine stood, glancing around for some clothing to cover herself before shaking off the urge to dress. She strode across the floor, furious at the interruption. Heaving open the door, she shouted, "I told you to leave me alone!"

But there was no one there. A faint smell of sulfur slapped her in the face and looking down, she saw a long, curved fang. It looked like it was from a beast, ripped out of its mouth so hard the pink gum was still attached, flowing with fresh blood. Bending down, Citrine touched the solid tooth, her heart thumping in her chest. Her vision went dizzy. She squatted on her doorstep, tears gathering at the back of her eyes as a truth struck her so deep she didn't want to believe it. "Zaul," she whispered.

14

KAI'S FOLLY

Kai snatched two slices of bread and a thick slice of cheese off the table, tying it into a bundle as she headed for the door. Mother was busy selling loaves of fresh bread, and Father was at the millhouse, dealing with his customers. They were both exuberant about these tasks, Mother talking too much and Father proud of the technical way the millhouse worked. He was brilliant with inventions, and Kai wanted to show him something special and unique.

Her memories returned to the shining orb. Citrine seemed pleased and excited, yet she ran off before Kai could ask her more questions. What if it was an invention, a power she could use the way Father used the waters to create grain from wheat? What could she create?

Hastily draining the cup of goat milk, fresh and warm from the pasture, she left the house. Each afternoon, she went to tend the goats with the other children. They would not miss her if she took a few seconds away to make sure the orb was still there.

She splashed through the cool waters, her toes clutching the rocks as she skipped toward the cave. Her cheeks bulged with bread and cheese. Before she entered the cavern, she peered back at the village, but Triften was knocking on the millhouse door and the villagers seemed to mind their own business. Satisfied they would not discover her, she swallowed the last of the bread and cheese and crept into the darkness.

The walls seemed to pulse, holding out invisible fingers as they welcomed their friend. She hummed as she moved, spellbound, toward the light, her heart lifting in awe as she stood before the beaming ball of light. It seemed to call to her, filling her mind and thoughts as she moved closer. Creeping forward, foot by foot, she held up a hand, daring to touch the orb like she'd seen Citrine do the day before.

The light pulled her in, shining brighter until she thought she saw tiny specks floating in the brilliance. What were they? Creatures of light? She brought her face as close to the orb as she could, listening to the hum of pleasure, almost like the purring of a beast. Gratitude spun around her like a warm blanket and she lifted a hand, questions rising on her tongue as she reached out to touch it. As soon as her hand touched the orb, it went numb and a suction pulled her in, close to the glowing beings as visions flashed through her mind.

Waves of light moved past her body like a current, pulling her in deeper. Glorious beings danced before her eyes and she heard a sound as sweet as morning dew above the purring hum. It was the song of the land, the tune that all living things carried through the ever-growing and flourishing land of Novor Tur-Woodberry.

A smile came over Kai's face and a peace settled in her heart as she listened. An understanding filled her mind and she felt as if two hands reached out and pulled her into an embrace.

Come, child, a voice whispered.

Anticipation mounted, and Kai opened her eyes wider as the floating specks took shape. The true mystery of the orb was about to be revealed to her. Just before the form took shape, she saw a black speck hovering in the distance. It hurled out of the light toward her face, and just as her mouth opened wide in a scream of terror, the spot turned into a fist and slammed into her forehead.

The blow hurled Kai against the cave wall where her head thwacked into stone. She crumpled to the floor, eyes closed with a trickle of blood flowing from her head.

15

CAPTURE THE FOOL

MORNING DAWNED LIKE A GIFT AS TOR LIR walked south, hiding in gray clouds of fog. His skin was cold and clammy from the chill of the night, and he brushed his dark hair from his forehead, finding it wet with dew.

He'd walked for a while that night after his bone-white companion forsook him, blending back into the shades of the forest as if she'd never appeared to him. An eerie puzzle lay before him. A strong premonition told him this was why he'd left the calm of the Shimla: to discover what mysteries lay in the realm of mortals and to fix them. The danger he'd told Lelia of was real, and he pressed on, searching for food, weapons, and a friendly person to talk to. He needed more information if he was to set free the bone-white creature and understand the motives of the Master of the Forest.

The life of the land flowed around him peacefully as

if ignorant of the torn body in the meadow and the struggles of the dark forest. It was, perhaps, midday when he came upon a wonder that made him stop in his tracks.

The white mist of the morning parted and before him rose vibrant green rolling hills. They reached to the height of mountains with rich colors glittering in the sunlight. Green bridges covered in vines melted with the enchanting blue of a sea-swept sky as he gazed upward. He swore he could see cottages perched on each hilltop and a windmill in the distance. A promise of Paradise hung in the air and the birds sang with the clarity of a pure sweetness.

Tor Lir shuddered at the powerful joy that hung over the land. His skin tingled at the idea of entering such a place. The potency differed greatly from the ambiguous mysteries of Shimla and the horrors of yesterday. He took a step, his foot landing in a patch of murky water. Scowling, he peered down and saw his reflection looking back at him, but what disconcerted him were the other faces he saw. Admittedly, there was the scurrying of footsteps across the land, and he'd heard them yet ignored them, assuming they were grassland creatures. Mice, rabbits, and weasels were common in the land, and he saw a red fox slink by. He'd thought nothing much of them. He minded his business and they minded theirs, but this time, he'd let his guard down.

"Get him!" a cry issued forth and a bearded male face rose, swinging a thick club.

"Wait," Tor Lir hissed, lifting a hand, aghast at his terrible luck.

The club smashed into his skull and bright motes sparked before his eyes as the green land turned upside down and his limbs went numb. "Why?" The question floated in his mind and burst out of his lips as bearded faces surrounded him.

"Bind his hands," one ordered.

"He's not out. Should we hit him again?"

"No, we aren't violent."

"Give him a moment."

Lavender hung heavy in the air and a bullfrog croaked in the marshes as Tor Lir's body was lifted. His neck fell back, and his eyes rolled up into his skull. He let the blackness take his vision while a low hum rose from the ground.

TRAPPED

THE WOODLAND CREATURES GASPED AND THE wind lady whirled into a volley of twigs and leaves as the shouts interrupted their conversation. Novor Tur-Woodberry turned to meet the creatures who had cried for help. "How may I assist?"

Two foxes, with their pointed ears laid flat, trotted up as if they'd been running flat out for a while. One had rust-red pelt, gleaming with beauty. The other had a rather dirty white coat with burrs hanging off his pelt. His feet were brown as if he'd waded through wet mud and it dried over, messy and crusty.

"Novor Tur-Woodberry." The red fox bowed his head in acknowledgment, deferring to the authority of the owner of the land.

"Where is Citrine?" the white fox interrupted, forsaking formalities. "I have a message."

Novor Tur-Woodberry considered a moment,

although the foxes did not seem menacing. Now and then, some dark creature would appear and find themselves powerless. The unspoken treaty of the land allowed no one to be harmed. "Try the cottage near the Standing Stones," Novor Tur-Woodberry told the foxes.

"I tried last night," the white fox rejoined. "It was empty."

The red fox stepped forward. "Have you seen her recently?"

"No." Novor Tur-Woodberry reflected on the fact that Citrine did not come to dinner the evening before. He'd sent a few of his Singing Men to request her attendance that evening. His thoughts turned suspicious: *What if she had something to do with the impending darkness?* He'd had questions before, but now he had many more. Perhaps she knew exactly who she was.

"I have an urgent message. If you see her, will you pass it along?" The white fox went on, its voice hard.

"Aye, go ahead." Novor Tur-Woodberry crossed his arms.

"Tell her. . ." The white fox paused, head down as he recited the message: "Zaul is trapped. The barrier is down. The Master of the Forest is coming."

"Humm. Trapped. Anything else?" Novor Tur-Woodberry scratched his beard. The title *Master of the Forest* rang like an ominous bell.

"That is all." The white fox dropped his head, sniffing the ground. "I must return to the forest. I have an exchange to make. Deliver the message. Don't forget."

The white fox turned tail and trotted off while the red fox pawed the ground.

"You have something to tell me?" Novor Tur-Woodberry prompted.

"The grass near the forest is . . . err . . . well . . . I think you should take a look," the red fox almost whispered. Then he, too, turned tail and ran off.

"As you were." Novor Tur-Woodberry waved to the expectant faces of the woodland creatures surrounding him. Taking his ax, he turned and headed toward the border.

AIR OF CLARITY

MIST SPILLED OUT OF THE BOILING KETTLE LIKE lavender fingers, pouring through the runes traced of ash. Citrine wrapped a cloth around the kettle and poured the water into a bowl, dropping leaves of lavender into it. Replacing the kettle over the fire, she dropped the fang into it. It fell with a hiss, dripping as it touched boiling water. Steam drifted through the air, causing the hair on her arms to curl up as she kneeled over the bowl. Bringing her face close to the heat, she breathed in while her breasts hung heavy and her nipples grazed the dusty floor.

"Air of clarity," she murmured, her lips almost kissing the trembling surface of the waters. "Grant me mercy. Allow me to see the memories taken. Give me eyes to see beyond. Recall the depths of the unknown."

She took a deep breath, slow and steady, allowing the scent of lavender to imbue her senses and let the worry drift away. *Zaul. Ava. Grift.* Concern regarding her beasts faded. Visions of herbs rose only to disintegrate even though she did not have the right concoction for the strongest potion. Closing her eyes, she let her senses envelope her. Fragrance filled her nostrils, and her eyes grew wet from the steam. A throbbing pulse drilled into her mind. One moment she was kneeling in her hut, the next she was back in the forest.

She held the skull in both hands while a bone-white creature led her between burned trees and a wasted forest. A drumbeat echoed in the distance and creatures howled in a mix of merrymaking and terror. Everything around her seemed hazy and blurred, and she thought she recalled swallowing something, perhaps when her head was underwater. She saw flashes of white and a leaping orange fire sang a song as it consumed the glade. Horned creatures danced, sharp teeth, red lips, and slobber flying out of their open mouths. The stink of rotten flesh offended her senses, yet she felt consumed and bewildered as she stumbled into the group of devilish creatures.

The creatures came to a halt when they saw her and the drums paused mid-beat. They peered at the skull she held in her hands, the terrible thing that made her feel cold with dread. A creature lifted a stick high in the air and howled, a terrible, high-pitched shriek that made her ears ring. They backed away, pointing from her to something amid the creatures, a hollow tree.

It seemed they wanted her to go into it and despite her misgivings, her disobedient feet led her toward the tree.

The trunk led down into darkness, a passageway of a sort, and even as she stepped foot onto the entrance, she knew where it would lead. She turned around in protest, but the bone-white creatures egged her on, stepping closer and shaking their sticks at her. Eyes darkening with veiled threats. Stretching out her leg, she took another tentative step . . .

The memory faded like a ripple across the pond, disappearing into nothingness. Citrine came to with a start, her legs burning from kneeling and water dripping off her face. Ignoring the bodily pain, she took a deep breath, understanding what happened. If she had to guess, she assumed the tree led underground into a labyrinth that connected to Novor Tur-Woodberry's land. Yet how she ended up in the middle of the land without the skull remained a mystery. She needed stronger herbs to bring back her memories, but in the meantime, she needed to speak with Novor Tur-Woodberry. An old ache began, closing her throat as she set back, cupping the bowl of now warm water in her hands. The last time she'd come clean and told the truth about herself, she'd lost everything. Love. Home. Life. Everything.

Novor Tur-Woodberry had been nothing but kind to her, but he might banish her if he discovered she had brought chaos into his land. She was unsure of his power—waves of it touched every inch of his land—but should he choose, he could make her life miserable again. For a moment, she regretted choosing to fight the Master of the Forest. It would be better for the villagers if she sneaked away in darkness, taking her beasts and fading into oblivion.

She poured the bowl of warm lavender water over her head, rubbing the scented liquid over her body as she washed away the grit. Standing, she wrapped a gown around herself, belting it at the waist and pulling on a light cloak. The arms were gone from the cloak, yet a wide hood hung down the back. She cast around for a knife. Finding her blade gone, or stolen by whomever had burglarized her hut, she flung open the door and strode out into the sunshine. She set her face with grim determination.

NAMELESS ONE

Novor Tur-Woodberry planted his ax, blade down, in the grass, and leaned on the long handle, his meaty hands twitching as a frown came over his face. A carpet of death stretched before him, ending in a patch of forested area. Angry trees marked the end of Novor Tur-Woodberry's land and the beginning of the Boundary Line Forest.

In all his years, Novor Tur-Woodberry had never seen such a sign as the one that marred his vision. The blades of once green grass were black and frozen as if someone had turned them to ice. Stepping on one shattered it into sharp shards, and dried blood hung on broken pieces where a creature had dared to walk and instantly regretted its folly. "So . . ." Lifting one hand, Novor Tur-Woodberry stroked his bushy brown beard, softened by the gentle oils he used to keep it shiny. "It has begun."

"Novor Tur-Woodberry, we've found a suspect." Jatoba's harsh tone carried across the bend. Novor Tur-Woodberry turned to meet the newcomers.

Five of his Singing Men strode toward him, two with firm grips on the bound arms of a youthful male. As Novor Tur-Woodberry's eyes fell on him, an understanding dawned. Visions of the future flickered through his mind, ever shifting as if they were not set in stone yet.

The male held a slight air of familiarity; he stood well over six feet tall with a slender, muscular body, unused to the trials and toils of mortals. His hair was obsidian black and hung rather long around his neck, hiding the pointed tips of his ears. His eyes were hard and flicked with an unhidden haughtiness. It was clear he disdained those who captured him. It was not an emotion Novor Tur-Woodberry could blame him for; there was no evidence against him causing the darkness in the land. Besides, as Novor Tur-Woodberry met his emerald-green eyes, he recognized who the male was.

"A suspect?" Novor Tur-Woodberry repeated the words of Jatoba.

"Aye, we found him wandering near the marshes, close to where we saw a dead body a few days ago."

Novor Tur-Woodberry glanced to the male who blinked, unsaid words lingering behind those stubborn eyes. Novor Tur-Woodberry noted the male's lack of vengeance to defend himself. It was an uncommon trait. Mortals were quick to blame and point fingers at others, accepting none of the responsibility, even if they were part of the problem. They never offered solutions. Mortals seemed locked in an intense battle to live life however they wished, free from repercussions and responsibilities. It was one reason Novor Tur-Woodberry had been sent to guard the land and keep it free from the ever-changing whims, chaos, and mischief of the mortals. The village was a new development, which became necessary after mortals settled on his land, content to live in Paradise after the hundred-year rule of the Black Steeds and the war between the mortals and immortals.

Novor Tur-Woodberry frowned. "Release the captive. We are on my land—there is no need for bounds."

"Aye, Novor Tur-Woodberry." Ash lifted a short knife and chopped the rope from the male's hands.

The male barely seemed to notice, his cold eyes fixed on Novor Tur-Woodberry as his arms dropped by his side. "Power surrounds this land. Is it yours?" the male asked, unaffected by the Singing Men's accusations.

"Oh ho," Novor Tur-Woodberry rumbled. "I am Novor Tur-Woodberry, and you have entered my land."

"Your *realm,* you mean," the male interrupted, his eyes moving toward the blackness of the grass. "You don't seem surprised to see me. In fact, if I could guess, it seems you recognize me. Why is that? And what has begun?"

Novor Tur-Woodberry felt rather than saw his Singing Men turn toward him, surprised at the line of questioning yet waiting, out of respect, for his guidance.

"Ho now." Novor Tur-Woodberry held up a hand, slowing down the male's questions. "You have many questions, and I have many answers for you. But my Singing Men have accused you of the crime of murder. Do you have anything to say about it?"

The male appeared thoughtful, his brows knitting together as he considered. "It's coincidence or a kind of setup. There are things in the forest"—his eyes turned toward the Boundary Line Forest—"and I'm curious to know more, but something is blocking me. Perhaps you know. What has begun?"

"Humm." Novor Tur-Woodberry turned his gaze back over the rigid grass. Blades stood frozen like a hand of ice waved over it, bringing an early winter. "The time of the immortals is over," Novor Tur-Woodberry rumbled on. "The war is over, a balance is coming to the world, and it is too much for me to stay here. My time is over. It is time for me to go."

The Singing Men turned toward the male, nodding as if they'd known all along. They were loyal without question, ready for the next phase in their immortal reign of the land.

"Where will you go?" The male's tone broke the tension in the air. "As I understand it, this is your land. Isn't that so? Who will own the land when you leave?"

"No one." Novor Tur-Woodberry lifted his ax from the ground and swung it over his shoulder. "But that is a discussion for dinner. Tell me, do you have a name?"

The male's emerald eyes became guarded, his voice

dipping into a gentle tone. "No. I have no name. Although I am called Tor Lir."

"The Nameless One." Novor Tur-Woodberry nodded as the pieces came together. For a moment, he felt a small nostalgia for the days of peace. He should have known, in all his wisdom, when Citrine set foot on his land, the days of peace were over. "Evening will be upon us." He motioned toward the impending sunset. "Come along—join me at my home for dinner. I would like to speak to you about your future."

The male called Tor Lir blinked. "My future." His gaze shifted to the black bladed grass. "I assumed we would discuss your land and what is happening in the forest."

A sudden merriment returned to Novor Tur-Woodberry's bright-blue eyes. "Aye, so we will, but you have a curious future. I have been waiting for you to appear in my realm for some time because I need to warn you. Someone wants to kill you."

LIGHTS OF THE VILLAGE

THE FLICKERING LIGHTS OF THE VILLAGE DREW Citrine's gaze. She saw them dancing high up, beyond her cottage in the shallows. She recalled the day Novor Tur-Woodberry showed her the village, offering her a temporary home until she regained her feet and moved on, as she desired. He made it clear there was no rush, yet she understood that one did not impend on his charity by staying in his home far too long. The notion of living with eleven males, no matter how gentle and jolly they were, did not sit too well with her.

Reluctantly, she asked for a home set apart where she could have privacy. Her original thought was to practice her art with herbs and runes. She needed time to gather ingredients and cast a spell of protection over her beasts so they could join her. Thoughts skated around the possibility of hiding them in the gardens as she once had. But it was clear that would not happen anymore. At the thought of her creatures, her mind set out a thread of communication, searching, hoping they were within reach.

Ava. Zaul. Grift.

There was no response. Chewing her lower lip, she eyed the lights, surprised to see them glistening when daylight still graced the land. The fireflies were larger than average and shone around twilight when the twin lights in the sky graced the land with an unknown splendor. Regardless, the village was on her way to Novor Tur-Woodberry's home, and she wanted to see the strange orb Kai had shown her.

"Citrine."

She jerked to a stop, spinning around, her heart thumping in anticipation. She relaxed when she saw it was only the budding oak tree that grew just outside her door. The Trespiral had left her shell again. Her slender body swayed back and forth in the late afternoon breeze. "I hoped you might come to visit me again." This time there was no joy in the Trespiral's face. "I've heard something odd today. A dissonance in the land."

"I know." Citrine nodded, a sigh passing from her lips. "I can't stay. I have to talk to Novor Tur-Woodberry."

"Then you already know about the tree?" the Trespiral asked.

Citrine cocked her head. "What tree?"

The Trespiral waved a shimmering hand in the direction Citrine had just come from. "One raven brought me word about a bone-white tree. It grows in the middle of the land. There's something odd about it."

Citrine felt as if two hands gripped her neck and squeezed. Her heart raced, and bile boiled in her belly. "In the middle of the land," she whispered.

"You look ill. Are you all right?" the Trespiral asked, bending forward with concern.

"Yes. N-no," Citrine stammered, her easy grace gone. "I have to go."

She gathered the length of her cloak in hand and turning her back to the village, ran, bare feet pounding through the grass. Shoes were not something she enjoyed wearing—even the soft leather boots that encased her feet like a blanket felt too controlling. She preferred her feet to be free to touch the true nature of the land and burrow herself in its arms.

Bile rose in her throat when she arrived at the place where she had woken and where, supposedly, she'd buried the skull. As she slowed down, her pulse pounding like the drums from her memory, she saw something white glimmering among the wild yellow-green grass. It was bone-white, a dirty beauty, soiled yet standing tall, a few inches above the tallest strands of waving grass. It had sprouted two tender arms, one reaching west while the other reached east.

Citrine's breath caught as she crept toward it while anxiety settled in her belly. Nubs on the tree showed where branches would appear, pointing north and south as they grew. They looked like tiny hands, lifting and pointing toward the sky, thanking it for life.

"I curse you," Citrine hissed, lifting her foot to kick it. Before she struck it, she thought better of her action. Leaning down, she gripped the slender trunk with both fingers and pulled, intending to snap it in half.

Nothing happened.

The cold of death folded into her fingers as she tugged. When at last she gave up and stepped back, her fingers shook from exertion and the tree stood as if she'd never touched it.

"I don't understand." She glared at it. "I am strong. I can break bone with my fingers. Why can't I break you?"

A piercing scream rent the air. Citrine leaped to her feet and spun around. She was sure the scream came from the village. Heart pounding, she dashed toward the sound, sprinting past her cottage and the bewildered Trespiral. Following the path that led up to the Standing Stones and on to the Mouth of Heaven, she let the echoes of the cry lead her on. Mischief. Chaos. It was all her fault.

MYSTERIOUS FUTURE

A JOLT PASSED THROUGH TOR LIR, AND HE
shivered. As soon as the giant spoke his name, Tor Lir
recalled he'd heard of the legendary land of Novor Tur-
Woodberry, the great and powerful Duneíthaír, from
songs the Iaens sung. His flight from Shimla made
sense. His purpose was to help the Duneíthaír keep his
land and the people of his land safe, yet Tor Lir was
unsure what role he was to play. He squeezed his fingers
into fists as he asked, "Who wants to kill me? How did
you know about my existence?"

"Come to dinner." Novor Tur-Woodberry strode away
from the blackened border. "We shall discuss . . ." His
boisterous voice echoed back and there was a laugh in
his throat.

A peacefulness came over the countryside, as if it had
been holding its breath, waiting for a cue from Novor
Tur-Woodberry. As the laugh rippled through the air, the

fear drifted away and a certainty of knowing, even though the future was inescapable, passed over the Land of Lock.

The Singing Men stepped away from Tor Lir, nodding with satisfaction. One began a low hum and words flowed from his mouth:

Novor Tur-Woodberry.

Novor Tur-Woodberry.

A hush of admiration swept across the land and a moment later, a multitude of voices chimed out in reverence and respect.

Novor Tur-Woodberry.

Novor Tur-Woodberry.

They sang of his great power, looping through the hilltops. The vast blue sky opened wide, welcoming their words. The song continued, singing of Novor Tur-Woodberry, his authority, and his benevolence. The Singing Men marched away, swinging their axes up over their shoulders as they set off, double pace, marching in rhythm to the melody.

Tor Lir watched them, surprised at the turn of events. One moment, he was their prisoner, the next, set free and invited to dinner while the song of the land weaved through him. He followed just as the Singing Men marched over a rolling hill and disappeared from sight. They moved in a different direction, away from the edges of the border where they'd led him to rendezvous with Novor Tur-Woodberry.

Tor Lir recognized the song as the constant hum he'd

heard ever since he entered the land, and he wondered if there were a hypnosis in it, compelling him to answer the wishes and whims of Novor Tur-Woodberry. Perhaps the animals and people who dwelt in the land were unaware it changed their minds when they entered, overcome with a certain peace because of the song that kept them there, powerless. He knew of his abilities, although the depths of his unique powers were unexplored. A shudder ran over his back as the word *Daygone* drifted into his mind, encouraging him to seek and find. He pushed the thought away and quickened his pace.

Eventually, a glade appeared, leading down a hill, sloping like the breast of a giant, coming to rest amid multicolored grass. A round cottage perched, shining in the grace of twilight. Tor Lir glanced west where the dual lights in the sky appeared. The sun and the Green Light, a beacon of hope. Legend told of a time before the Green Light appeared in the sky when the world was dark with evil and hopelessness stained the ground with the blood of those who fought on the side of good. When the Great Conqueror arose, he set the Green Light in the sky as a beacon of hope, reminding those that their lives were not doomed and they had a chance in the war between the mortals and immortals.

It was a grandiose tale, but Tor Lir had no reason to believe it or disbelieve it. The Iaens loved to tell stories, truth and untruths spilling from their lips without consequence. Tor Lir saw their need to speak and astonish others, yet he knew even amidst the lies, each story held a spark of truth. If he could filter the layers of untruths, he would find the true meaning.

A spark flashed as the green and gold beams of light collided and Tor Lir walked to the doorstep. Fragrant flavors brushed his senses, making his mouth water as he realized the extent of his hunger. He'd not had a proper meal since leaving Shimla, and in his curiosity, the bits of snatched meals were unsustainable.

His eyes widened as he stepped over the doorstep, surprised to find himself graced in a forest of golden light. There were no walls in the cottage, only great tree trunks, rising to form a canopy of green leaves with golden filtered light as the ceiling. Long grass grew up around the trunks of those trees, swaying back and forth as if there were an unknown wind, or perhaps they danced to the unceasing music of the land.

A tingling came through the air, dancing on the edges of Tor Lir's vision and disappearing before he could quite grasp it. Out of the corner of his eyes, he thought he saw a grand castle with chambers, staircases, and rooms disappearing into a void, but it was only his imagination.

"Welcome," Novor Tur-Woodberry boomed, appearing at the door, holding a pipe. He held out his arm, his hand pointing toward an oak table in the middle of the room. It sat twelve, and ten of the seats were full with more of the stout, four-foot-tall males. A few of them sent curious glances toward Tor Lir but seemed content to wait for food before diving into a conversation.

Tor Lir ignored their glances as he moved toward the table, feeling shabby, but when he looked down, his clothes were crisp and clean as if he'd never had a tussle with a beast in the wood. What kind of power was this?

"Have a seat, eat and drink," Novor Tur-Woodberry said. "And when you are full, we shall have a discussion, for we have many things to talk about."

Tor Lir felt as if they had enchanted him. He opened his mouth, but not a word left his lips as he sat down at the table while the melody of harps filled the air. His plate filled itself with an abundance of everything at the table while the goblet perched by his plate shone with a golden liquid. Mounds of food covered the table, from stuffed pig to gourds of fruit dripping with cream to roasted vegetables. Crusty pies perched in front of each plate, the flakiness melting in his mouth.

When at last he'd eaten his fill, he sat back and found time drifted away while the tastes and smells of the glorious home of Novor Tur-Woodberry consumed him. He relaxed in his chair, which had become deeper, almost pulling him into the realm of slumber. He wondered if it had seduced him, and part of him did not care at all. He sank into the glory and beauty as his mind sent warnings cavorting into the void.

The smell of tobacco woke him from his trance and he sat up, noting the roaring fire. Novor Tur-Woodberry sat closest to the fire, his booted feet stretched toward it while the golden light flickered on his bushy beard. His Singing Men surrounded him, holding either goblets or pipes, enjoying the whimsical music that brushed past their ears.

Tor Lir straightened up, heat coming to his cheeks as he wondered how long he'd been out of it and what power he'd inadvertently let Novor Tur-Woodberry hold over him. Questions regarding the truth of the legend of the great Duneíthaír stirred in his mind and he opened his mouth as clarity returned. "You mentioned that I have a mysterious future and someone is trying to kill me. Care to elaborate?"

Novor Tur-Woodberry met his gaze. The merriment left his eyes, replaced with a calm seriousness. He puffed on his pipe a minute longer before taking it from his mouth to answer Tor Lir's question.

21

BRIGHT AND SNAPPY

"I ASSUME YOU KNOW THE OLD STORY," NOVOR Tur-Woodberry began, settling back in his chair, his deep eyes gazing into the fire.

Tor Lir could see some age in him then, through the eyes of someone who'd lived hundreds of years. Respect came over him, for the creatures he knew in Shimla were young and restless. Youth made them unintelligent, and boredom gave way to petty spats full of drama.

"Over nine hundred years ago, the Creator designed the Four Worlds, giving life to mortals, immortals, plants, and animals alike. In the beginning, all teemed with life and yet there still were blemishes in the land. The Creator had a mischievous assistant who distracted him during creation, causing the Changers to morph from the Creator's spark."

Changers. Tor Lir shifted at the word, a prick in his mind telling him he should understand. The aura of the word emitted a strange darkness, and part of him wanted to know more while the other part of him wanted Novor Tur-Woodberry to skip that story and move into deeper reasonings.

"During a time of chaos, the Creator sent me to this land to bring balance to the divide between good and evil. He gave me a specific power to watch over and guard all living things in this land. Blessed with wealth and wisdom, I made this haven where all that is great and good may dwell and flourish without fear. Since the land is vast and butts up against the Boundary Line Forest, I was also given ten Fúlishités, also known as Singing Men, although there are no men in this realm. As the power of the Changers grew stronger, I recognized the break in my gift. As long as the Fúlishités and I stay on this land, we receive power. If we leave, all immortality and unique abilities are stripped from us. But we are content here." Novor Tur-Woodberry's eyes twinkled. Raising his pipe, he puffed on it for a moment, replenishing the air with the heavy scent of tobacco.

Tor Lir mulled over the words and came up with two questions. Before he could ask them, Novor Tur-Woodberry faced him, pointing a pipe at Tor Lir's face. "Now you are here. The Nameless One. The Balancer. Tor Lir. You shall have many names in your lifetime, but now it is up to you to keep the balance between good and evil."

Tor Lir narrowed his eyes, words spitting out of his mouth before he had time to consider whether it was a worthy question. "How do you know?"

Novor Tur-Woodberry raised an eyebrow, a chuckle on the edge of his lips. "How could I *not* know? Wisdom and knowledge are imparted in various ways. I felt the shift when you entered my land—just as you see and understand auras, I acknowledge the knowing of the present and future. You may assume history is created by those who strive to make a difference in the present, but that is not so. It is only a recurrence of the past, with a different location and a new spin on truth. There are many things I know that would astonish you. I must hand them to you in bits and pieces, for you are young and do not understand the depths of the realm of mortals. Yet."

Tor Lir examined Novor Tur-Woodberry, letting the hostility fade from his eyes, recognizing he needed a mentor, someone knowledgeable to look up to. "I understand your truth now, and I would like to sit at your feet and understand the depth of knowledge. Will you teach me? The realm of mortals is new to me, and it would relieve me to have a guide as I make my way."

Novor Tur-Woodberry stroked his beard. "To recognize your lack of knowledge is wise. Yet I am not the guide you seek. You cannot learn the lessons of life here in my land—this is Paradise, a guarded haven. If you want to understand the realm of mortals, you must go beyond my land to seek truth. I feel you already know where to go to find the knowledge you seek."

Daygone. The word jetted through Tor Lir's mind as if it had been said out loud. He almost jumped out of his seat as an uneasiness swept through him. "I see," he told Novor Tur-Woodberry. "Why does someone want to kill me? I've only just left my former home, and I have met no one on the way . . . except for the strange creature in the forest yesterday. Why does someone want me dead?"

"It's not you in particular. It's the idea of you," Novor Tur-Woodberry said. He held out a hand as he returned to his pipe, signaling the need for a short smoke break.

Smoke rings from the Singing Men drifted above Tor Lir's head, fading into the shimmering curtain at the end of the room.

Tor Lir settled back in his chair, just as a *tap-tap* came through the walls. Three knocks and then a boom sounded as if a foot kicked the hidden door.

"Oh ho, what is this?" Novor Tur-Woodberry rose from his chair, taking the pipe from his mouth. "Ah, let her in." He spoke to the hut as if it were alive.

"Novor Tur-Woodberry," a female voice called out. It was not a pretty sound; her voice rang with impatience as the hut opened invisible doors to let her in. "I have something urgent to tell you . . ." She trailed off as she entered.

Tor Lir rose in surprise as he took in the unexpected guest. Waves of bright hair tumbled around her shoulders in vibrant colors impossible to pin down. As the light shifted, the color of her hair changed from blonde to red to orange, hints of black and silver running through her roots. He saw her aura shimmer and snap around her as she glared at him.

She was surprisingly tall for a female, about six feet, with a heart-shaped face and a well-endowed body. Her lashes were long, and she blinked at him out of eyes the color of a rare jewel: citrine. Her lips were full and almost pouted as she glared at him, her jeweled eyes shifting from examining him to questioning Novor Tur-Woodberry.

A sleeveless, loose frock fell to her knees while a longer cloak covered the rest of her body. Given her height and the coloring of her skin, Tor Lir assumed she must be of the people group called Tiders.

When she placed her hands on her hips, he saw the curves of her body and a twitch of lust pierced him. It wasn't affection, only desire. She was attractive and desirable with a hard heart and a quick tongue. There was something about her he could not quite name. Her aura danced and weaved through the air, sending scattering thoughts toward him like a shield.

"Who's he?" she demanded, pointing an accusatory finger at Tor Lir. "I didn't know you had a guest."

The way she spoke seemed as if she were the mistress of the land and should be informed when newcomers appeared. She frowned, her lips turned down as her skirts switched around her legs. Tor Lir noticed she was barefoot and looked as if she'd run wild in the wind.

"This is my guest," Novor Tur-Woodberry explained,

as if the female's words did not bother him. "Come along, I will introduce you. We already ate dinner, but if you are hungry—"

The female snapped her fingers with impatience, cutting off Novor Tur-Woodberry in a hasty manner. "Nay, just wine." She paused, licking her lips before adding. "Please." Glancing again at Tor Lir, she turned her entire body toward Novor Tur-Woodberry. "I came to speak to you about something urgent."

"Aye, join us then. Urgent business seems to be all we discuss this day."

The female lifted an eyebrow in disbelief. "What do you mean?"

"Sit," Novor Tur-Woodberry boomed at her, an undercurrent of laughter bubbling up. "You are impatient today. Sit and drink, then we shall speak when you have a moment to organize your thoughts."

The female looked as if she might utter another rude word but thought better of herself and plopped down with a sigh, holding out her hand for a golden goblet of bright-red liquid.

22

LAWS OF BALANCE

CITRINE GLARED AT THE LANKY MALE AS SHE took sips of the bold wine. It tasted rich with hints of chocolate on her tongue. A calmness came over her, greater than the feeling the scent of lavender gave her. The male's emerald-green eyes were cold and emotionless as his gaze lingered on her, as if she were some unwanted refuse in his path. He was young with long black eyelashes, an angular face, and roughly cut black hair. If he had the hints of a beard, she might think him handsome, but the vibe she got from him was eerie and unusual.

She couldn't place him among the people groups, either. There were four main people groups in the South World. Crons, a people group of a short stature and a fair complexion known for their lust for adventure. Tiders, such as herself, who lived at great heights given their long and limber bodies. Trazames, who were farmers, and Ezincks who were dark-skinned and preferred forests. In the future, Citrine hoped to find a tribe of Ezincks and study with them. Their healers crafted unusual spells from herbs, and Citrine knew some spells she'd forgotten were from the Ezincks.

She took another sip of wine to keep her frustration from rising and to avoid blatantly staring at the male. He was tall like a Tider and something about the way he sat, holding his shoulders straight and examining her with his emotionless eyes, made her feel sick. Her heart beat faster and her fingers twitched in discomfort. She couldn't pin down what it was, but she did not like him.

His eyes left hers and returned to Novor Tur-Woodberry, who sat back in his chair, stroking his great beard while the firelight highlighted the gold in his rich brown hair.

Citrine felt her heart turn over as she looked toward Novor Tur-Woodberry. When her eyes drifted back to the male, she saw the perfection in his body and a slight glimmer. In the firelight, it looked like a faint pale-green shimmer surrounded him, almost unseen in the flickering light. Shaking herself from her unorthodox observation, she returned to the task at hand.

"Novor Tur-Woodberry." She addressed him with respect. "I've just come from the village. Kai, the miller's daughter, went missing today. The villagers spent all afternoon looking for her. She was wandering in the caverns and fell and hit her head . . ." She lapsed off, glancing at the green-eyed male, wondering how much she should reveal with him here. "I'm sorry." She broke off. "I can't talk with him here." She pointed an accusing finger. "Who are you?"

"This is Tor Lir," Novor Tur-Woodberry rumbled, speaking for the male as if defending him. "I'll allow him to answer your questions."

Citrine lifted her chin as she met the cool gaze of the male. "I suppose that's not your real name."

His eyebrows lifted in surprise. "Why do you say that?"

Citrine shrugged, somewhat cowed. "I only assumed, because it was the topic of a recent conversation with a Trespiral." With a huff, she turned back to Novor Tur-Woodberry. "We don't have time for this. I need to speak with you. Alone." Her eyes begged him to adhere to her request.

"Tor Lir is not used to the realm of mortals, and he is seeking a guide into the world." Novor Tur-Woodberry addressed Citrine, ignoring her request. "I believe you would be the right guide to show him the way of the world."

"A guide!" Citrine leaped to her feet, aghast as she glared from Novor Tur-Woodberry to Tor Lir. "I can't be a guide! Who do you think you are?" She glared at Tor Lir, baring her teeth.

His eyes were cold as he met hers, a semblance of hostility just behind them. "I come from the forests of Shimla, the haven of the immortals. I uphold the balance between good and evil. Something is wrong here, and I will discover what my role is in mending the uneasiness gripping the land."

Citrine sat down hard, all the air going out of her at his words. She examined him from head to toe again as memories of her flight through the Boundary Line Forest consumed her. She recalled a dream, or what she hoped was a sleep-soaked dream, of white creatures with lidless eyes. Forgotten words pressed on her memory. *"There is an imbalance between good and evil. Her actions will help keep the balance."*

"What about him? His purpose is to keep the balance."

She shuddered, her voice coming out just above a whisper. "Who are you then? If you're not a mortal?"

A flicker of uncertainty appeared in his cold eyes, which shone like jewels. Citrine shivered, reminded of the legend of Treasure Hunters, Jeweled Ones who wielded extraordinary power once they found the stone that matched their eye color. Surely Tor Lir was one. "I'm not sure yet, but I intend to find out."

His words sounded like an omission of truth. Citrine watched him shudder, a smirk almost coming to her face, yet she caught it in time. She held up a finger. "To clarify, you were born among the immortals and you lived there until you left?"

"Yes," he assured her. "I have a purpose I will complete. And who are you? If you are to be my guide, I'd like to know more about you." He grinned at her, a cunning grin, like a wolf.

Citrine sat back, reaching for her wine and taking a

sip to avoid looking into those odd eyes. She sneaked a glance at Novor Tur-Woodberry as she pulled the goblet away from her lips. A drop of red wine dripped down onto her lap, staining her bare leg with its juice.

"My name is Citrine. I am . . ." She paused, for her speech was not prepared and she was unwilling to share her true nature. "New to this land," she finished.

"Where were you before you entered this realm?" Tor Lir leaned forward, his deep eyes inquisitive.

"It's not a realm," Citrine snapped, somehow annoyed with him. He was cold and uncaring, and she did not want to look at him again lest his coolness seep into her skin. Yet all the same, her eyes examined his angular features as if chiseled from stone. She could not help but wonder who he was and what kind of power he held. "I came from a village beyond the wood where they cast me out."

It sounded strange admitting that truth out loud.

"Why were you an outcast?" Tor Lir's eyes turned dangerous, and she did not want to talk to him anymore.

"Perhaps it is time to turn the conversation to things at hand," Novor Tur-Woodberry interrupted, rescuing her from dark thoughts of the past. "Tor Lir, please explain what led you here, aside from your intuition. We can return to our previous conversation another time."

Citrine detected a hint of disappointment in Tor Lir's eyes. However, he opened his mouth and smooth words poured from his guileless lips. She leaned toward him, curious about him as he spoke. He related his journey south from Shimla, elaborating when he discovered a dead body and was chased by a strange beast into the forest. Citrine raised her eyebrows in disbelief when he talked about the bone-white creature that came to him and led him out of the forest. Only, he was captured by the Singing Men and taken deep within Novor Tur-Woodberry's land. When at last he finished and his lips grew silent, Citrine found her fingers gripped her chair, as if something froze her in place. A horror wormed its way around her, and despite her thoughts, she could not help but assume it was her fault the land of Novor Tur-Woodberry was in chaos.

Before she could speak, Novor Tur-Woodberry took his pipe from his mouth and stared into the flickering yellow tongues of fire. "It is as I thought. My time is over, and I must leave because the world is at peace and I am not required. The land will miss me, but they don't need me."

"What?" Citrine shrieked, the scream dying in her throat at the terrible words from Novor Tur-Woodberry. Tears rose in her eyes, unbidden as she stared at the Singing Men. Their expressions were somber as they stared at the fire, nodding one by one as if they regretted knowing the truth. "But you can't go," Citrine begged, her fingers turning white. "Your land is a haven. What will happen when you leave? Evil is rising to take over this land. Are you going to let it?"

Novor Tur-Woodberry took his pipe from his mouth

and faced her, his eyes deep with kindness and understanding.

But it was Tor Lir who responded as if a vision graced his mind. "The great war is over. There is a shift in the balance, but too much goodness abounds and leaves no room for chaos. If peace is to last in this world, then this sanctuary, this Paradise, must perish. All is good and great in this realm—a land such as this is not needed."

Fury rushed through Citrine at Tor Lir's words, and she wanted to reach out, find his neck, and wring it. Her fingers twitched, begging to do her will and bring misery to the emotionless, uncaring guest.

"There was a time when I hoped this land would always be kept by a powerful Duneíthaír, but I cannot see the future." Novor Tur-Woodberry spoke up, his voice calming Citrine's murderous gaze. "The land is ripe for chaos, and I feel the time is now. Tor Lir is right. My time is up."

"What will happen to this land and the people who live here?" Citrine wanted to shout and scream and cry all at once. How dare they take Paradise from her. How dare they let this happen to the land when they had the power to stop it.

"The land will die." The bleak truth dropped from Novor Tur-Woodberry's lips and a somber air filled the room.

"Can you stay longer?" Citrine whispered, her face a mask of sorrow. A heaviness dragged her down as her world caved in on her once again.

"My time is at an end." Novor Tur-Woodberry lifted his pipe, puffing methodically as he stared into the fire.

"What of the Creator who sent you here? Surely he will grant you grace," Citrine pressed, setting her goblet of wine on the arm of her chair in a precarious way.

"Perhaps. There are bigger matters at hand than the beauty of Paradise. Perhaps because of the peace, my land is not needed."

"No," Tor Lir interrupted. "It's because of the balance. There is none. Since the war, the balance has swung to the side of good and there it rests. We need chaos in the land, or it will end. The fall of a great land such as this will bring balance."

"Who cares about balance?" Citrine demanded, glaring at Tor Lir, ready to rip his tongue out. "There are people who live here!"

"I care about balance. I am the keeper of balance."

"Why does it matter!"

"Because there must be order."

"Why?"

"It's why I have come. I don't know why. I have a strong feeling."

"Can't you change the balance?"

"Change? Why would I change the laws of balance?"

"To save this land!"

"I can't just come in here and change the balance. There must be equality between good and evil."

"No. There shouldn't! Isn't that why the White Steeds fought the war? Not to bring balance and equality between good and evil but to save life. Why won't you save the land? Why won't you risk it?"

"It's not my purpose."

"Well, maybe it is and you're so befuddled with propriety you don't know it yet!"

"Perhaps there is a way," Novor Tur-Woodberry mused. "Citrine, my time is over, but we can still save the people. Although Paradise will fall, we can halt evil. I invited you here for a reason tonight because I know you did not enter this land by chance. Perhaps now is the time to share with us what you know."

23

WHAT CITRINE KNEW

Ava. Citrine reached out for threads of connection. *Come.*

"What are you doing?" Tor Lir's question broke her concentration. "You look like you're talking to someone."

Citrine frowned at him, her heart pounding. She took a deep breath, meeting Novor Tur-Woodberry's kind eyes. Would he cast her out if she told him the truth? Would he do what her past lover had done? "I am an Enchantress." Saying the words out loud somehow made it true, and she realized she was proud of her secret heritage.

"*The* Enchantress," Novor Tur-Woodberry stressed, encouraging her to continue.

"Did you know?" The strength of her voice dropped away as she held his gaze, awe and wonder at the respect in his eyes. There was no hate and no need to drive her away while burning everything she cared for.

"You have a unique future, but my vision is not clear," Novor Tur-Woodberry went on. "However, I know you are the strongest Enchantress who has ever lived. Much like Marklus the Healer was the greatest healer of all time, standing between life and death."

"Pardon me," Tor Lir said, a glimmer of curiosity in his emerald eyes, and something else that seemed like lust. "What does that mean? What abilities do you have?"

"I am a friend to nature," Citrine explained. "I have a unique bond with it. I respect nature, and it hears and answers my requests. I understand how to use the various plants and runes for healing, knowledge, and other skills as required. I also have beasts."

"You control beasts?" Tor Lir stared at her in surprise while Novor Tur-Woodberry and the Singing Men fixated their gazes on her.

The room grew silent, the quiet music in the background fading away. Only the flickering fire provided the slightest noise.

"*Collect*. I collect—not control—them and they obey my wishes. It is respect for respect." She was sure Tor Lir understood nothing about respect, and her lip curled at him. "I only collect exotic beasts with the same eye color as myself."

"Citrine." Novor Tur-Woodberry took his pipe out of

his mouth. "There is something special about your gift. What else happened to you in the forest?"

Citrine paused, reaching out for more threads of communication. *Grift. Get out of the forest. Come to Paradise. It's too dangerous.*

There was no response.

"I've seen this happen before," she admitted, speaking to Novor Tur-Woodberry. Vulnerability rose and the words she'd refused to tell another living soul came spilling out. "It happened in the village I lived in before I came here. Crops were dying, animals turned up dead with strange bite marks, and children disappeared. The villagers were superstitious—they blamed me and drove me out. But it wasn't my fault . . ." She trailed off. Her tone sounded desperate and defensive. It felt wrong to defend herself among the first who gave her the decency of believing her story. At least, she hoped the respect in Novor Tur-Woodberry's eyes meant he believed her tale.

"Do you know what happened to the village after you left?" Tor Lir asked.

Citrine shook her head, her eyes darkening. "No. And I don't care." The lie left her lips too quickly, and she dropped her gaze to the fire to keep her chin from shaking.

Memories took her back to her flight through the forest, and when she hid in a hollow log to rest. White beings with snakes for hair and tentacles for arms stood where she had rested. They spoke of things she did not understand. Narrowing her eyes in memory, she sought to recall their words, but they were lost to her, just like her memories the night she buried the skull. Since nothing came back to mind, she spoke the words she knew would change everything. "I met the Master of the Forest."

Tor Lir leaned forward. Citrine recognized the lust for adventure dancing in his eyes. He desired a quest and a purpose for his life. He wanted an escape from the humdrum and to dive into something exciting and bigger than him. He desired knowledge and praise and something else she could not quite put her finger on. "The bone-white creature told me it serves the Master of the Forest. And you've met him?"

"Yes." Citrine lifted her chin, answering the unspoken challenge.

"Under what circumstances?" Tor Lir asked.

"I was lost in the wood. I made a deal with him to help me find a way out."

"Of the forest?" Tor Lir crinkled his forehead in disbelief. "I'm sure you would have found a way out."

"Are you judging me?" Hot blood rushed to her ears. "You have no place to judge when you were lost in the forest yesterday and had a bone-white creature lead you out. You don't understand my circumstances!"

"Aye." Tor Lir held up his hands, signifying peace while his emerald eyes laughed at her temper.

"Tell us more," Novor Tur-Woodberry interrupted, soothing the air with his questions.

"I followed a river, you see . . . because of my ability to tame monsters. One of them told me where to find the Master of the Forest."

"Why didn't you tame the Master of the Forest?" Tor Lir's eyes glinted as if he could pull her thoughts from her mind.

Citrine frowned at him, her tone becoming hard again. "My abilities don't work like that. The Master of the Forest is an undead creature. He . . . it . . . can't be tamed. There are certain circumstances my abilities cannot transcend."

"Interesting." Tor Lir sat back, still watching her. "How do you tame your beasts?"

She didn't want to talk to him, and yet, she did. It was an odd feeling and a combination of relief at being able to talk about her unique gifting. "It's all free will. I establish a metaphysical link with them and we communicate in our minds. They swear allegiance and then they are mine."

"Perhaps the Master of the Forest is the same way." Tor Lir cocked his head. "Perhaps that's how he bends the forest to his will, and we must take that ability from him. Perhaps he means to take it from you."

"I very much doubt that." Citrine denied the thought, terrified she considered it. Tor Lir's words would ring true. "If he wanted my power, why did he let me go? He asked me to cause chaos wherever I go." She bit her lip as soon as the words left her mouth, but it was too late. Surely they already knew the chaos in the land was her fault, and when they discovered she'd buried the skull that gave the Master of the Forest more control, they'd drive her out.

"Chaos is only a distraction," Tor Lir mused. "There's something deeper he wants. What is here? What does this land have that no one else has?" With his last words, he turned to Novor Tur-Woodberry.

Novor Tur-Woodberry nodded as he spoke. "Here, there is the power of good without evil. Peace without chaos. And the song of life that holds this world together. My land and the Boundary Line Forest are opposites, planted side by side to keep the balance. Yet all has changed now, and I do not blame you." His eyes twinkled at Citrine, understanding her anxious thoughts. "Citrine, can you find the Master of the Forest again?"

Citrine closed her eyes, going back to the moment and reaching out. *Morag.*

Citrine. The tone was hollow in her thoughts.

You must leave, she begged.

We cannot speak this way.

Why not?

Trust me. Come.

Are you by the river?

Aye. Be warned. If you come, there is no turning back.

I do not leave my beasts.

So you say.

She broke off on the unkind note. Novor Tur-Woodberry waited while Tor Lir examined her as if he'd like to pry open her skull and take her abilities. She shuddered, curious about what power he possessed, especially if he was not mortal. "If we can find the river again, I can find the Master of the Forest." Although she wished no such thing, the Master made her skin crawl. She did not want to meet him again.

"I would like to go with her to find the Master," Tor Lir said to Novor Tur-Woodberry.

"What will we do when we get there? You don't know what he's like. What if he tries to kill us?" Citrine snapped at him, her temper rising. The look on his face said he thought it was all an elaborate game.

"We will determine what happens when we get there. Don't you have beasts you need to set free?" Tor Lir rejoined.

"Yes." Citrine glanced to Novor Tur-Woodberry for help.

"Let's leave in the morning," Tor Lir suggested. "In the meantime, are the people of this land safe?"

Novor Tur-Woodberry rose to his feet. "Leave the people of the land to me. They are my responsibility. You two must assist with something else. This is why you've come to my land. If my Singing Men and I leave, we lose our power. We cannot go to the forest and confront the Master of the Forest, but you can; and if you want to help, it is your quest. I have gifts for you, for the forest is deep and treacherous and you are not prepared to face monsters with what you have now."

Citrine took a long sip of wine. There was more she

wanted to say, especially about the light Kai showed her and the bone-white tree growing in the center of the land. She was unsure how to proceed with the odd male in their presence. More than anything, she desired a word alone with Novor Tur-Woodberry before she forsook his land.

The Singing Men hummed the dark tune to a ditty, and harp music struck up in the room. The roaring fire burned lower, and the room shifted into a cavernous hall.

"Follow me," Novor Tur-Woodberry said. Reaching up, he pulled a latch behind the fireplace and opened a massive door into a cool hall.

24

HALL OF WONDER

TORCHES FLICKED INTO BEING WITH YELLOW lights pulsing on either side of the yawning hall. A wide stone path led into the darkness. Citrine gazed in awe at the endless cavern, stretching onward and moving upward without end. She crossed the threshold, cool stone gracing her bare feet.

"I did not know this place was here. From the outside, your small cottage does not look like it hides a treasury," she exclaimed in surprise.

Novor Tur-Woodberry chuckled. "There are many mysteries you haven't seen yet. Rare circumstances require visitors to see the treasury, but you have come here unarmed. I have no choice."

"I thought I saw vague shapes flickering when I came down the slope," Tor Lir admitted. "Is it unusual to have a home like this?"

Citrine snorted. "You have much to learn about mortals."

"Lack of knowledge does not mean I am unintelligent," Tor Lir reprised her, his eyebrows drawing together, stopping just short of a frown. "I am quick to learn and understand, but everything is new. I don't know yet."

"Nor should you, but you have a mind open to knowledge, so you will gain wisdom." Novor Tur-Woodberry admonished Tor Lir as he led the way down the stone path.

The torches seemed to light themselves as the three moved forward and extinguished themselves when they left the direct path of light. When Citrine looked up, she was sure she saw faces in the flames, staring at her.

"Those are the flame-creatures," Novor Tur-Woodberry explained, his deep voice echoing off the walls. "They prefer to live down here, coming and going as they please. There are only ten, which is why the lights go out behind us. They are flying ahead to light our path."

"Like the Iaens of Shimla who light the glade for the great dance," Tor Lir murmured.

"Aye, like that," Novor Tur-Woodberry agreed.

Citrine frowned, feeling left out of a mysterious secret. "What are Iaens?"

Novor Tur-Woodberry glanced to Tor Lir, inviting him to answer the question. A guarded look came over Tor Lir's face, as if he did not want to speak. "Iaens are secretive. I am not sure how much I should relay to you," he answered.

"Are you afraid I'll use your knowledge to barter?" Citrine snapped, irritated. "I trusted you with my greatest secret—perhaps that was a mistake."

"Tor Lir, I would encourage you to speak freely with us, but to guard your secrets with others. As your gut tells you, we seldom know the motives of mortals. You would be wise to be careful who you trust." Novor Tur-Woodberry turned toward Citrine. "Iaens are the immortals of Shimla. As a whole, you may hear them called Iaens or Idrains; however, there are different species. For example, the Green People were influential in the war between the mortals and immortals."

Citrine noticed Tor Lir's eyes narrow, but just as quickly, all expression left his face. In the flickering lights, it seemed as if she had imagined it.

"There are many other species," Novor Tur-Woodberry continued. "A few include the Rainidrains, the Falidrains, and the Jesnidrians. They each are unique, just as the four people groups of the Four Worlds have their unique traits. There was a time when the Iaens grew in number and were abundant throughout the land. Since the war, they keep to themselves, hidden in forests, no more to bind their fate to the mortals."

"What species are you?" Citrine asked Tor Lir, her curiosity about his history piqued.

"I am all," he said, his eyes remaining on the torchlight, the reflection glowing in his green eyes, like the

Green Light and the sun at daybreak. "I am the first and last of my kind. There is no one like me. That is all I will say." He shut his mouth into a grim line and his eyes darkened.

"Eh, you both shall have plenty of time to discuss later, I wager." Novor Tur-Woodberry nodded at them as they approached a flight of winding stairs. "Watch your step—we descend to the treasury."

"Novor Tur-Woodberry, I would like to point out, amidst the interruptions you never explained, who wants to kill me?" Tor Lir asked, his voice muted against the walls.

Citrine jumped at the unexpected question, her heart beating faster as she trailed her hand over the wall, hugging close to it. The other side of the staircase was wide open, a precarious place to fall to, what she assumed would be, her death.

"Aye. What I have to say is for both of you, but concerns you, Tor Lir. Citrine, because you travel together, you must be aware." Novor Tur-Woodberry's voice turned grave. "This message concerns your future, a joint future regardless of what takes place here. There is a zealous sect, a spin-off of the Order of the Wise and the Wise Ones. As you know, the Order of the Wise died out long ago, although the descendants of the Wise Ones still live and breathe. After the war between the mortals and immortals, watchers and rulers took up reign in the west. Their purpose is to guard against the rise of the immortals and keep those with great power from abusing the freedoms of the mortals. They call themselves Disciples of Ithar. They search for individuals with unique powers and take them, keeping them under guard so they cannot release chaos and war on this world. There may come a time when they find out about you and seek to kill or consume your knowledge and power. Watch out for them."

"Disciples of Ithar?" Citrine felt a mixture of fear and anger roaring within her. "Who came up with such a terrible idea?"

"Terrible?" Novor Tur-Woodberry asked. "Seek to understand, and you will know. You did not live through the war, during a time when the power of the immortals was unleashed and they wrought a great massacre on this land. They slay all the elders of time, leaving only the youth who lack knowledge to pick up the pieces. There was only one wise enough to see beyond their conniving actions: King Idrithar of the Torrents Towers. Alas, he disappeared ten years ago and there is no word of his whereabouts. Only his disciples follow in his legacy, and there is a reason for that."

"A reason?" Citrine snapped, losing her temper at last. "There is a reason they seek unique people with unusual powers and try to kill them? That is evil!"

"There is much good and evil left in this world. How you will navigate the dark desires of mortals and balance the greater good is up to Tor Lir now. I beg you, as situations arise, seek to understand from all sides before choosing. Remember, life is precious, but deception is abundant. In choosing to save many, you may destroy the entire world."

"Certainly it is not as deep and drastic as you make it seem?" Citrine asked, cowed before Novor Tur-Woodberry's great knowledge and power. Someone who'd lived hundreds of years would know more about the world she lived in. Her twenty-five years seemed short considering Novor Tur-Woodberry's years. She turned to Tor Lir, realizing she wanted him to agree. Silence met her. There was a dark glint in his eyes, and she could see he was considering Novor Tur-Woodberry's words.

Novor Tur-Woodberry chuckled as they approached the bottom of the staircase and the torches around an archway lit up. "Do not fear, but beware, for darkness surrounds us. We are all given a choice to choose between darkness or light. It's a choice I want you to know of, regardless of where your adventures take you. I can only tell you so much—you must take the words I have given you and choose what kind of action you will take in life."

"You sound as if we are going away forever." A sorrow pierced her heart, and she reached out, intending to touch Novor Tur-Woodberry's shoulder. She felt a deep yearning to stay in the land and remain in Paradise. "I only want to go to the forest, find the Master of the Forest, and return here, to stay with you."

Novor Tur-Woodberry turned to meet her gaze and his eyes were gentle. He nodded at her. "I understand your desire." Then turning, he lifted a ring of keys from his belt and unlocked the arched door. It swung open with a creak and pure air flowed out. The torches gave a little shriek of joy as they went dark and the flame-creatures rushed to light up the room.

Citrine felt her heart drop and her eyes fell to the stone floor, examining them as if they had rebuffed her. Someone had carved a myriad of intricate runes into each square block of stone and covered the treasury with a rich history spun with imagery. Citrine's eyes widened as she examined the treasury. She'd never seen one before and had nothing to compare it to, but as with everything else, the home of Novor Tur-Woodberry held its own secrets.

Tor Lir walked to the middle, turning in circles as he examined runes while Novor Tur-Woodberry drew up beside Citrine. "We will speak more after this," he murmured. Citrine could not decipher whether his words carried a promise or a dig for more information. She scratched the back of her neck, wondering if he knew she hadn't been completely truthful with him.

The treasury was a circle with glass walls at each corner, which created round turrets where cases of weapons and armor hung. There were long swords with curved blades, short knives for hunting and skinning, and great axes for cutting. Some weapons were simple while others were decorated with gold, silver, and mysterious runes. There were long bows and arrows with colored tips, boots made of leather, and shields hammered into squares and curved shapes. A heartbeat of power centered in the middle of the room, thick with a warning against the misuse of the weapons there.

A waist-high rectangular block sat in the middle of the treasury with an ax carved out of marble and riddled with runes resting on top. Novor Tur-Woodberry walked toward the block. Running his thick fingers down the broad side, he grabbed a latch and pulled. A drawer opened, a row of short blades lay inside, some with straight edges, others with curved edges. "Now tell me, what kind of weapon do you prefer?"

"I've done well with the bow and arrow," Tor Lir said, gazing at quivers of arrows hidden behind a wall of glass.

"Bows and arrows are for cowards." Citrine couldn't help the jab that slipped from her lips. She moved to join Novor Tur-Woodberry. "I prefer knives."

"You look as though you prefer hand-to-hand combat," Tor Lir remarked as he joined Citrine and Novor Tur-Woodberry.

"I'm not afraid to get my hands dirty," Citrine retorted, unsure why she let him ruffle her feelings.

"Weapons are given for different reasons." Novor Tur-Woodberry held up a hand. "If the two of you argue like children, you will not achieve your goal. A bow is called for in case someone attacks you from afar while knives are better if anyone sneaks up on you." He lifted two blades, the length from his wrist to elbow. The blades were curved while the handle was a deep ivory, almost white. "Citrine, there are grooves in the handle that make it easier to grip. See what you think of these."

Citrine took a knife in each hand, considering the weight and balance. Holding the blades toward the gray stone floor, she backed away. A hot rush poured through her veins as again she recalled the Master of the Forest, the buried skull, and Zaul's fang. Anger roared through her and a piercing cry echoed through the air as she lifted the blades over her head and twirled them with her fingers. She stamped her foot, fighting against the urgency to run and rip everything from its place. A fierceness came over her body and her eyes narrowed as she returned the knives to their neutral position, blade down. "Yes, I would like these." She returned to the block where Novor Tur-Woodberry took the blades and sheathed them into cases of leather.

He handed her a belt, a twinkle coming to his blue eyes. "They are yours."

She smiled at him before recalling Tor Lir was with them. The glow faded from her cheeks as she watched him study the runes on various weapons. "What are these?" His fingers traced the rune on the handle of a knife.

"There is a rich history of lore associated with runes and symbols." Novor Tur-Woodberry reached out a hand and ran his fingers over the ax. "Citrine is familiar and attuned to the ways of nature. Alas, we do not have the time to discuss further tonight. For now, pick a bow and arrow for your journey, and a hunting knife. Your chambers await you."

Tor Lir gave a quick nod as Novor Tur-Woodberry handed him a bow and quiver of arrows. He tucked a knife into his belt as the flame-creatures hustled to the archway, their voices whispering into the night. Citrine watched them, and a cold shudder went down her spine. Closing her eyes, she reached out with her mind, seeking her beasts.

SILVER-WHITE HEART

THE WIND HOWLED. NOVOR TUR-WOODBERRY raised his eyebrows in concern as he held open the door to a chamber. "Tor Lir, rest here tonight. The sunshine will wake you and you may be on your way to the forest on the morrow."

Tor Lir nodded at him and then Citrine before entering the room. The door swung shut behind him, leaving Novor Tur-Woodberry and Citrine alone. "Come," he beckoned to her, sensing the anxiety that churned through her. "You wanted to speak with me?"

Citrine opened her mouth, a retort about to fly from her stubborn lips. Yet instead of speaking, she returned to the fire and curled up on a chair. Tucking her feet under her, she leaned forward and rested her chin in her hands. Novor Tur-Woodberry sat across from her.

"There was a message for you," Novor Tur-Woodberry began, rubbing his hands together. They felt empty without the comfort of his pipe, but he'd smoked enough for one day. "A pair of foxes brought them, one white, one red. Do you know any foxes?"

Citrine shook her head, her jeweled eyes guarded as she waited for bad news. She seemed to sense it coming and steeled herself against the impact.

"They said to tell you that Zaul is trapped, the barrier is down, and the Master of the Forest is coming. What do those words mean to you?"

Citrine blinked, fury behind her eyes. With one slender hand, she moved strands of bright hair away from her face. Novor Tur-Woodberry noticed that in the flickering firelight, her vibrant hair took on a rather orange color. She shrugged. "I've already told you. I made a deal with the Master, and now he is coming for your land. I don't understand why, and we already have a plan in motion to stop it."

"Is there nothing else?" Novor Tur-Woodberry leaned toward her, gathering the hints of lavender that lifted from her body. There was something she wasn't telling him, confirmed by the way she dropped her eyes and shifted her gaze to the fire.

"Nothing else." She fell silent, fidgeting with the hem of her dress. "I don't understand." Misery replaced her bravery. "This is your land—you are the most powerful being here. How can the Master of the Forest threaten you? You've been here for hundreds of years."

Novor Tur-Woodberry sighed at the question. "Like I told you before, the balance is shifting. Things are different now. I perceived there would come a day when I was no longer needed in this land, and it would be time for me to go. That time is now."

He felt a bittersweet nostalgia as he said the words once again, and the thought of leaving and going to his final resting place brought a sense of peace.

Citrine bent her head, her hair hiding her face from him before she shook herself out of her reprieve. Her eyes were shining when she looked at him, and he noted the stubborn tilt of her chin. "Kai, the miller's daughter, showed me something in the caves, a big white ball of light, and it spoke to me."

Novor Tur-Woodberry sat up fast, his eyes widening at the surprising statement. "It spoke? What did it say?"

"I can't recall. But Kai went to see it today and something attacked her. She's at home, sleeping, but I think the villagers blame me. They saw me go to the caves with her yesterday and they believe it's my fault."

"Hmmm . . ." he said.

"Novor Tur-Woodberry, what is that light?"

Novor Tur-Woodberry shook his head. He was both surprised and concerned the light appeared to Citrine and spoke to her. A brief debate rippled through him. He wanted to explain to her, and yet, he also wanted her to tell him the truth and stop hiding her knowledge.

"Kai called it the Silver-White Heart," Citrine continued, raising her eyebrows as if to encourage him to speak. "I saw something in it . . . something dark."

"What did it say to you?" Novor Tur-Woodberry

asked, scratching his beard. The fact that the light appeared to the people of his land was a dire warning. He understood his time was at an end, but now the people of his land were in danger from more than one source. The Master of the Forest was coming to take Paradise while Paradise itself was dying.

Citrine bit her lip, her eyes roving back and forth as if she were searching for something. "I can't remember all of it," she admitted, shrugging. "There was a voice that spoke of the end of times and the Creators. I remember that part clearly because I was surprised it said Creators as if there is more than one. That's not true, is it?" She leaned toward him, sending a wave of lavender to his nostrils.

"Aye, you are a sharp one," he murmured. "There is deep knowledge in the Four Worlds and if you seek wisdom, you shall find it. If, indeed, there is more than one Creator, it is only because there is more than one world."

Citrine shuddered. "You speak of life beyond the Four Worlds? As if there could be such a thing. Impossible."

"Hum . . . you cry impossible, and yet, you do not know all. It is possible the Four Worlds is all there is to this universe, just as it is entirely possible there are worlds beyond our imagination. If you seek wisdom, you must not make accusations based on your limited knowledge. Those who are wise understand this truth. We do not truly perceive unless we humble ourselves, ask questions, and keep our minds open to possibilities."

Citrine scowled.

Novor Tur-Woodberry could only imagine she was not used to being rebuked, no matter how kindly he placed his words.

"Never mind all that, I forget myself." He reached out his hand to pat Citrine's, and she flinched. "To answer your question, the Silver-White Heart is the heart of this land. As long as the light is whole and pure, my land will remain. Yet you saw a darkness in it?"

"Yes." Citrine's face reddened. "Is it because of the Master of the Forest?"

"It is a coincidence I will investigate tomorrow." A yawn caught in his throat and he closed his eyes momentarily, listening to the gentle voice of sleep ready to pull him into the beyond. "The hour grows late, and you must be tired."

Citrine folded her hands in her lap and looked down at them, avoiding his gaze. "Nay, I need to prepare for this journey into the forest. You gave me weapons and I thank you for it, but I also need herbs, food, and water."

Novor Tur-Woodberry waved a hand to reassure her. "No need to worry. I will have my Singing Men pack supplies for you and Tor Lir. All shall be ready for you at dawn."

Novor Tur-Woodberry noticed Citrine twitch when he said the name *Tor Lir*. She looked up at him, her eyes narrow. "If I may speak plainly, I don't like him." She bit her bottom lip before proceeding. "He's arrogant, and he only just arrived here. He doesn't care about the land or saving it. I don't understand why he's here or what his purpose is." She held up a hand to keep Novor Tur-Woodberry from protesting. "He's here to keep the balance between good and evil, but he doesn't seem to care about anything other than the balance. He doesn't understand or respect the land, the people of the land, or the animals. Why would he put his life in danger to save it? In fact, I *know* he won't put his life in danger to save your land . . . "

She trailed off, blinking and swiping at her eyes. Novor Tur-Woodberry saw the depth of her commitment to the land and something else. She turned her head away from his and back toward the fire. "I don't want him to come with me. I can do this by myself. If you will provide supplies, I'll leave tonight."

"Citrine," Novor Tur-Woodberry said, coaxing her to understand why she needed to travel with Tor Lir. "He is new to the realm of mortals. He does not understand yet, which is why I want you to be his guide. Take him through the realms. Show him what is priceless. Perhaps then he will grasp what you and I already know regarding life in this world. He does not understand his true purpose nor does he know who he is yet."

"And you do?" Citrine whispered, still blinking hard.

"Not quite," Novor Tur-Woodberry mused into the fire. "There is some truth to what he says, but he does not understand the entire revelation."

Citrine lifted her chin. "I don't know if I can make him understand—"

"Nay, that is up to him. All you need to do is show him the way. I believe you would do well with him by your side, if not to your benefit, then for his." Novor Tur-Woodberry rose and stuck out a hand to help Citrine to her feet. "Are you willing?"

His fingers closed around her warm hand and he held it a beat as he waited for her answer. Citrine glanced down, noticing their joined hands, and her expression changed. Novor Tur-Woodberry thought he saw a glint of triumph in her light eyes as she faced him. She opened her mouth and said the words he'd hoped she'd say.

26

STRAWBERRY DAWN

TOR LIR WOKE TO THE SOUND OF WIND CHIMES, and a roar rushed passed his ears. He sat up, surprised he'd slept at all. Generally, he did not sleep, but his mind needed to absorb the information he'd learned last night. Swinging his feet over the down-feather bed, he pulled his pants, shirt, and jerkin on. Wiggling into his boots, he straightened his clothes and slung the bow and arrows over his shoulder.

At the last moment, he noticed a dark cloak resting on the foot of the bed, as if a silent stranger had crept into the room at night and placed it there. Curious, Tor Lir ran his fingers over the material. It was soft, well-kept fur. A shudder passed through him as he lifted the garment and flung it around his shoulders. A sigh of peace escaped his lips as he donned it and strode back and forth. The cloak hardly weighed anything and floated behind him as if it were his shadow. He ran his fingers through his hair and glanced around for a door. An archway appeared and striding over, he reached for the ornate door latch and swung open the door.

A gust of wind hurled through the outer room, swinging the door to the chamber back with a boom. Tor Lir jumped and peered out into the main room, raising his eyebrows at what he saw. The wind blew into a vortex, turning from transparent nothingness into something solid, out of which stepped a female. She was as tall as Citrine and her skin, brown as an acorn, had a honey-like glow about it. A gown the color of a cloudless sky moved around her body as if caught in a faint breeze. She turned her bright eyes on Tor Lir, examining him before asking, "Are you a guest of Novor Tur-Woodberry?"

"Aye." He nodded, his heartbeat quickening as he realized the room had changed once again. Golden light bathed the room, capturing the first light of sunrise. A table sat against the wall with steaming piles of baked buns, fruitcakes, and pies while baskets of fruit—strawberries and blueberries and pineapple—covered almost half the table. Tor Lir's mouth watered at the sight. The lands of the Iaens were abundant in fruit, and the sweet tang of nostalgia moved through his body. "Who are you?"

"I am the wind lady," she offered. "I have come with a gift, but first I must deem this land worthy of such a gift. Tell me, have you been here long? What are your views on Novor Tur-Woodberry and the inhabitants of this gracious land?"

Tor Lir paused. The wind lady's face appeared open and frank, and yet he felt his guard come up. "If you don't mind"—he bowed slightly, for her presence seemed to demand it—"I am just passing through and Novor Tur-Woodberry was kind enough to offer me hospitality."

"Is that so?" The wind lady smirked at him. "I thought I saw you tied up and led by the Singing Men. Yesterday?" She touched a finger to her flat nose as her bright eyes laughed at him.

Tor Lir scratched the back of his neck, moving closer to the fruit. The inviting smell of freshly baked food hung in the air, different from anything he'd ever experienced. The creatures of Shimla did not cook their food and ate what bounty of the forest they could forage. "Err . . . well . . . it was all a misunderstanding. I am leaving now."

"Are you leaving because of your impression on the land?" the wind lady queried. "I ask because . . . I want to know. The more I gleam from first impressions, the better I can choose whether this land deserves the gift I bring it."

Tor Lir pondered her words as he popped a strawberry into his mouth. A burst of flavor awakened his senses, and he sighed. A wave of homesickness passed over him at the taste and more than anything, he missed the wild gardens of Shimla. The youths among the Iaens harvested the gardens, and it was a duty he enjoyed until he grew old enough to graduate from harvesting. The Iaens saw hard work as a punishment or a disgrace. Only new Iaens or prisoners were given the task of harvesting the bountiful gardens.

Raising his eyes to the wind lady who watched him eat, he thought of a proper response. "This land is a beautiful haven." He spread out his arms to indicate the whole of the land. "But something is wrong. The land is dying. I don't know what your gift is, but at a time like this, it is either much needed or will be in vain."

The wind lady considered him, emotion fading from her face. "See, that wasn't so hard, was it?" Spinning, she turned to stride toward the door just as Citrine burst into the room.

Citrine glared at the wind lady and Tor Lir watched them eye each other like two lionesses prepared to pounce on each other and defend their territory. The wind lady's lip curled as she examined Citrine, and she opened her mouth as if she were about to speak. Citrine was faster and cut her off, turning her back on the wind lady and angling her body toward Tor Lir. "Are you ready?" she demanded.

Tor Lir was surprised to see Citrine fully dressed for travel. Dark boots that came to her knees clad her feet. They looked as if they were made of the hide of some creature. She still wore the short shift that fell just above her knees, but her cloak was longer. On her back was a pack—full of food, Tor Lir assumed—a bedroll, and a waterskin. She had fastened the two knives given to her by Novor Tur-Woodberry around her waist.

"Aye." Tor Lir ate another strawberry, reveling in the sweet flavor for a moment before straightening his shoulders. "Where is Novor Tur-Woodberry?"

"He rises at dawn to survey his land." The wind lady laughed as her winds blew through the room, gathering strength.

"Ah." Tor Lir noticed the scathing look Citrine gave the wind lady before turning on her heel and flinging open the heavy door. It swung out, showing them an emerald sunrise, invading the land.

Tor Lir turned toward the wind lady as Citrine marched out the door, her strides long as she headed southeast. He placed his palms together and bowed in her direction as a farewell, unsure what else to say about the mysterious home of Novor Tur-Woodberry.

By the time he turned around, Citrine was a quickly retreating figure, moving in a blur. He broke into a run to catch up with her, curious about his guide but sensing words were not welcome.

27

INTO THE FOREST

THEY WALKED SILENTLY FOR A WHILE. CITRINE let the sting of seeing another female in the house of Novor Tur-Woodberry fade away like an old wound. She understood he had many guests, yet after their conversation that evening, she'd felt an unusual closeness to Novor Tur-Woodberry. Finding another female in his home made her feel as though she'd read into the situation more than she should have. Eyeing the exquisite male by her side, she let her curiosity override her misgivings. She opened her mouth and words tumbled out, no need for hesitations or politeness. "Novor Tur-Woodberry weaved magic into our cloaks," she told him, wondering if he already knew.

Tor Lir raised his eyebrows, tilting his angular face to examine her. His green eyes seemed deep and unreadable. "How?"

Citrine stuck out her chest, proud she knew something Tor Lir did not know. "Novor Tur-Woodberry's land is vast and wide. Depending on where you start, it could take days to cross it and enter the Boundary Line Forest. But Novor Tur-Woodberry and his Singing Men can move through the land at will . . . almost like—"

"They control the ability to move through portals within their land?" Tor Lir interrupted.

Citrine paused in surprise as she considered his words. "Yes, like that," she agreed before walking forward again, quickening her pace as her dark cloak swished around her bare legs.

"How do we use the power?" Tor Lir's voice had an enchanting lilt to it, as if he could break into a song and a sweet melody would pour out. Citrine wondered if he persuaded those around him to do his bidding without regard for morality.

"I'll do it." Citrine stopped again, unwilling to share all of her knowledge with him. When she looked at him, her eyes wanted to slide away and for a moment, she could have sworn she saw a green glimmer. "Come stand by me and touch my cloak. Then close your eyes and empty your mind."

A slight grin came to Tor Lir's face. "It sounds as if you will put a spell on me." He moved to stand in front of her, placing both his hands on her shoulders.

Citrine felt an instant moment of uncomfortableness at their proximity. Although she was almost six feet tall, Tor Lir stood about a head higher than her and smelled of pine and honeysuckle. She breathed in as she closed her eyes, almost tasting the fragrances that surrounded him. Spicier aromas rose from his chest, a blend of cedar, cinnamon, and juniper. It was intoxicating. She wondered what it would be like to press her lips to his skin and if she could taste the flavors there. The herbs of the forest seemed to stick to him like burrs. She hadn't noticed his distinct smell in the house of Novor Tur-Woodberry.

"You look as if you're enjoying this," Tor Lir interrupted her thoughts, laughter in his voice as he squeezed her shoulders.

Citrine's eyes snapped open, and she lifted her chin. "You're supposed to have your eyes closed. Stop staring at me—you're ruining my concentration."

"I know little about spells, but I don't think you're supposed to smile," Tor Lir murmured, his voice dropping to just above a whisper.

"You wouldn't know, so be quiet," Citrine scolded him, but there was no anger in her voice, only a bittersweet wistfulness. She closed her eyes again and visions of dark-chocolate eyes and a teasing mouth rose before her. *Let the past be the past.* She rested her hands on Tor Lir's arms and turned her thoughts to the Boundary Line Forest, recalling the bone-white creature, the skull, and the glade where they met in.

A sharp wind flickered around her and the stinking scent of sulfur entered her nostrils. Wrinkling her nose, she opened her eyes and let go of Tor Lir. Something crunched under her feet and looking down, she saw grass as sharp as ice and black like obsidian.

"May I open my eyes now?" Tor Lir squinted as he peeked through one half-open eye.

"Aye, we're here." Citrine nodded as she turned, her eyes drawn to the stretch of blackness in front of murky trees. A strong odor accosted the land and thick trees rose before her, cutting out all daylight.

"This must be the Boundary Line Forest," Tor Lir stated, folding his arms across his chest.

Citrine scratched her head. "We are standing at the border of the land of Novor Tur-Woodberry. His power can only take us this far, but . . . something is wrong. Why is the green grass dying?"

"Ah, you haven't seen this? It's happening across the land, I assume. I was in the marshes yesterday when I saw the darkness bubbling up from underground. When I met Novor Tur-Woodberry, he was standing in front of the grass. It's sharp as a knife, so be careful where you step."

"How can the Master of the Forest have this much power?" Citrine stomped across the charred grass toward the trees in frustration. "Don't you see?" She glared at Tor Lir. "We need the balance to swing in favor of Novor Tur-Woodberry. Paradise is dying. Don't you care?"

"It doesn't matter what I think," Tor Lir replied, his expression aloof.

"You made your point clear last night," Citrine said,

not caring how rude she sounded. "All you care about is the balance between good and evil. There is no such thing as balance, and if there is, there shouldn't be. You are new to the realm of mortals, but what you should care about, above all things, is life and sustaining life."

Tor Lir was silent and Citrine wanted to slap his face. His green eyes slanted and his cheekbones were high. She could see the shadow of a future beard, but then they ducked under the trees and his features blurred into the darkness of the forest.

The air, stinking like rotten eggs, was thick and dim as they strode through the forest. They moved in and out of boughs, Citrine tripping over underbrush and cursing under her breath at their slow speed. As she walked, she reached out feelers of communication, seeking her beasts, a gnawing worry eating away at her, at their silence.

Ava. Zaul. Grift.

There was no answer.

After a while, she eyed Tor Lir, seeking something to distract her from worrying about her beasts. Regardless of what she thought of him, an aura of mystery surrounded Tor Lir and since fate seemed to toss them together, she might as well find out more about him. "You don't seem to know very much about yourself," she remarked, her words piercing the stillness of the forest. "Who are your parents? What powers do you have?"

"I don't want to know. I think the cost outweighs the

knowledge." Tor Lir shrugged as he navigated through the wood as if he were born there. His footsteps were silent, and he moved with a quick and easy gait.

"What an odd thing to say." Citrine lifted her hair off her neck as she sweated. "Everyone wants to know who they are, because it defines your life and gives you purpose and meaning."

"You're wrong," Tor Lir replied defiantly. "My past doesn't define my life. I decide who I am and what gives my life meaning. I don't need dark secrets of the past to define me. I want to start out fresh with clean thoughts. Those secrets might be evil. There is no need to discover them."

"But don't you want to know? How can you run away from such knowledge? What if it unlocks the key to your power?"

"What do you know of my power?" Tor Lir's tone turned cool like a frosty winter.

"Not very much, and neither do you," Citrine retorted, refusing to look at him. "You're like an invisible person—you're here yet you're not. You don't have a personality. You are cold and curious and you don't care about anything. Novor Tur-Woodberry asked me to be your guide, but I don't know if I can because you are impossible."

"Impossible?" Tor Lir asked. "What does that mean?"

"You're difficult!" Citrine snapped. "You're hard to understand and unchangeable. Do you know what? I think you might possibly be evil, and you might turn against me when we meet the Master of the Forest. You might even be on his side—"

"I am not evil." Tor Lir's voice turned to a low growl and his arm shot out, gripping Citrine's upper arm.

He yanked her around to face him, his grip like iron, forcing Citrine to stare up into his face. She expected to see a furious scowl, but his face was calm, his eyes unnaturally cold as he glared at her. "Ever since you saw me, you looked at me and judged me. When the first words left my tongue, you examined them and found them lacking. I saw the look on your face. You disdain my companionship and think you are better than me when you don't know who I am. Don't take me for mere appearances and don't judge my character before you know who I am. I am many things, but above all, I am not evil," he stressed.

Citrine knew she had struck a nerve, and the look in his eyes terrified her. She felt as if a cold mist settled in her throat, forcing the breath out of her. She gritted her teeth, torn between yelling at him to let her go and egging him on. "I can't trust you," she whispered. "Because you won't talk to me. I don't know who you are. I don't know if I can trust you. Talk. Tell me who you are."

He let go so suddenly that she almost fell on her backside. Stumbling away, she leaned against a tree, her fingers wrapping around the green vines of the trunk for protection. He glared at her a moment longer before his eyes changed, the coldness drifting away like the sunrise scattering the shadows of night.

"I will try. Walk with me. I will not harm you."

Citrine peeled herself away from the tree, leaving a wide gap between her and Tor Lir. Her heart thudded in her chest as she rubbed her arm, wondering if she were walking with the enemy.

ORIGINS

"THE FOREST OF SHIMLA IS MY BIRTHPLACE," Tor Lir began in his lilting voice as if he'd never threatened her.

Citrine rubbed her arm as she walked behind him, glaring at his backside and wishing she held his bow and arrows. He'd shown a brief instance of his temper and she was tempted to do the same. A warning arrow that nicked his ears would be worthy repayment for the bruise he'd left on her arm.

"I hear most mortals are born." Tor Lir glanced back at her, and Citrine refrained from making a face at him. "That's true? And you know your parents?"

"Mmm," Citrine hummed between her lips.

"It's different for the creatures of the wood. Most of the Iaens aren't born from each other. There is a place called the Birthing Grounds where flowers bloom with the seed of an Iaen, bringing them to life full-grown. It is the place where all knowledge and memories are kept and shared among the Iaens."

"Strange." Citrine couldn't help but interrupt. "Are you saying all Iaens are born with knowledge? How come you claim you know little about mortals?"

"I don't know how to explain it to you and I don't know if I should. Iaens have their own knowledge they pass from one to another just as mortals do. During the war between the mortals and immortals, all of the Iaens left, taking their vast knowledge with them. Now we have no ancestors to glean wisdom and understanding from—all the wise ones are gone. I was born the first of my kind, the beginning of a new era, one without knowledge of mortals and how they dwell. Instead of learning the world at large, Iaens are taught how to protect ourselves, the lore of old, and what to do if mortals enter our realm."

"Those three things are the most important?" Citrine asked, not intending to be snobby, but it came out that way.

"What did you learn?" Tor Lir glanced back at her, a hand on a thick tree trunk. A lock of hair fell onto his forehead, making him look younger and less severe.

"Independence, the lore of nature, and . . ." Citrine paused. Her upbringing was uncommon. Her parents were hard and relentless and taught her to be the same. Citrine had taken on her mother's features, including her vibrant, ever-shifting hair color and curvaceous body while she had her father's eyes and long limbs.

Citrine the Enchantress, her father called her, his eyes glowing. *You have a natural gift to call the beasts to yourself. Be wise and use it for good. There will be those who seek to use your gifting for their own benefit. It's smart if you keep your knowledge to yourself, even if you should take a mate. In this moment, we hope that the war between the mortals and immortals may end. Regardless of what happens, there is a reason the Creator has given you your gift. There will always be good and evil in this world, and perhaps you may have a hand in the smaller events that take place in your lifetime. Always remember who you are and always remain in control of the voices.*

Citrine squared her shoulders as she recalled the words of her father, and regret poured through her. She should not have opened her mouth and told Novor Tur-Woodberry, let alone, Tor Lir, who she was. Some secrets needed to remain buried, and she'd already jeopardized her family name by blabbing. Holding her tongue and keeping her temper were recurring mistakes in her life.

"What did you learn?"

Tor Lir's question brought her out of her memories and she blinked at him, dismissing his question. "I learned how to take care of myself. There's no hereditary knowledge for the mortals. My parents taught me everything I know. What were your parents like?" She threw the question at him, sorry she'd talked about herself.

"I don't know," Tor Lir mused, apathetic. "A green giantess raised me. She left this world when I was ten."

"Oh, I'm sorry," Citrine responded, unapologetic. She

wondered how he handled the death of his guardian at such a young age. "Do you miss her?"

Tor Lir paused before turning to face her, a strange expression crossing his face as if he were not there at all. "This is why I don't like to speak about my past. There are many conflicting thoughts and feelings. I don't miss her and yet I feel as though she is part of me and her legacy lives on through me. She was a queen and she built a magnificent kingdom, willing me to do the same. The words she impressed on my memory will not leave me alone."

Citrine felt the fingers of unease grip her at his words. Tor Lir walked back to her and leaned forward, his eyes narrowing as he examined her face. "What is it about you?" he whispered. "You entice me to bare my soul. Do you enchant everyone you meet?"

Citrine took a step away from him, her heart hammering as if he had given her an unwelcome kiss. "You're a king?" she echoed. "A powerful king of the immortals?"

"Nay." He shook his head as he swept his black hair out of his face and tucked it behind his ears. They were large ears and pointed at the end, clarifying his odd breeding. "I am no king, and I will not take up the legacy left by those who came before me. I came to keep the balance and choose my own fate."

Citrine took a deep breath and for the first time, she saw an unnamed emotion in Tor Lir's face. If she had to describe it, she would call it fear. "You're running away from something," she blurted out. "As long as you stay away from the Iaens and their knowledge, you can keep running and never look back. Keeping the balance is only an excuse."

Tor Lir grinned, his eyes lighting up and his teeth flashing for a brief second. "Aye." He winked at her. "You are quite perceptive. If I had to guess, I would say the same about you."

Citrine frowned. "I'm done running. I will face the Master of the Forest." As the words left her lips, she saw an arrow streak out from the corner of her eye. Acting on impulse, she leaped, hurled herself at Tor Lir, and bowled them into the thick underbrush of the forest. Twigs snapped under their bodies as an arrow slammed into the tree trunk above it, pursued by two more.

Tor Lir's lips moved beside Citrine's ear, tickling her with his warm breath. "Someone wants to kill us."

29

MONSTERS AND MAYHEM

CITRINE'S LEFT HAND CURLED AROUND THE handle of her knife and yanked. "Let me up." She pushed Tor Lir's shoulder off her chest. "I will fight back."

"Are you sure that's wise?" Tor Lir whispered.

"Don't be a coward," Citrine hissed. "You have a bow —arm yourself. The creatures of this forest are evil, and they will not hesitate to slay you." She rolled over and scrambled to her knees, pushing her cloak out of the way, cursing as it snagged in brambles.

"We can't fight what we can't see," Tor Lir protested as he lay flat on his back in the underbrush where she'd left him.

"Hush," Citrine interrupted as a high-pitched chirping came from above her. Raising her head, she narrowed her eyes at the dense foliage, unable to see what was up there.

The chirping grew louder and faster until a piercing shriek and a thrashing sound came from the treetops. Citrine fumbled for her second knife and planted her feet as leaves and twigs rained down on her head. She held a hand over her eyes, shielding them from the onslaught. A blur of brown-and-white hurled out of the tree, screaming with murderous rage. A pointed stick whistled overhead.

Citrine yelled and swiped back, her knife striking the midpoint of the stick and snapping it in half. The creature screamed and tossed both ends at her and then leaped for a tree branch, scaling it and disappearing from view in a matter of seconds.

"Ha!" Citrine shouted, shaking one of her knives at the tree.

"Bah!" the creature yelled back, tossing a handful of leaves on Citrine's head.

"Come back here, you rascal," she shouted, kicking the tree. The impact jarred her toes and she cursed. She wanted to climb the tree, but when she reached for an overhanging branch, her hand slipped away and was covered with a sticky substance. "Sap," she whispered just as the chirping sound rang out again.

Two creatures assailed her this time, beating about her head with a stick as they dived from the tree.

"Tor Lir!" Citrine shrieked, ducking the assault and flashing her knives back and forth, missing each time as the creatures hopped around her. "Where are you?" she demanded.

Another stick snapped in half, and she spun as two more creatures hopped down from the tree, leaping over brambles and bushes as they charged her. Her knives sliced, but she wasn't quick enough. Two feet slammed into her back with such force that she fell over, crashing into the underbrush, almost cutting herself on her knives. Holding her arms out, she landed roughly on her fists and tried to climb to her knees. Before she could rise, a creature hopped on her back and another pinned her arms to the forest floor, snatching at the knives she clasped in her fist.

"Get off me, you oaf!" she shouted, her temper rising. "Let me go!"

Something landed on her head with a *thunk* and her head slammed into the ground, searing pain surging between her eyes. Blood poured from her nostrils and for a moment, she couldn't catch her breath. She kicked her legs as hard as she could, even as she felt a noose wrap around each ankle and then tug, pulling her legs apart. A curse rose in her throat and she opened her mouth, gasping for breath and spitting out leaves and dirt. A stick smacked across her back and she tried to lift her head, only to feel a heaviness land on it and push her back down. Her nose smashed into the ground and her breath came short and fast. Fury rose within as she sent out threads of communications to her beasts.

Help. Ava. Zaul. Grift. Help me.

The silence was not encouraging and at last, she willed herself to be humble and called upon the latest beast in her collection, the one who had not proven himself true. *Morag. Help me.*

A stick walloped her back, breaking skin. Citrine hissed in pain as other sticks slammed into her arms and legs. She arched her back, attempting to use what measly strength she had left to wiggle free, but the pressure on her head made it difficult to breathe. She fought, her fingers clawing at the dirt while her legs yanked against the rope. Despite her struggles, she could only pull in shallow breaths. Darkness flickered around her eyelids and a sensation of drowning made her struggle once more, but they held her fast.

Bile rose in her throat and she choked, blood and snot spewing from her nose as the creatures continued beating her. Her fists relaxed, and the knives fell out of her grasp. A moan escaped her lips and while the burning fire in her belly told her to fight, the creatures bested her. There was nothing to fight for anymore.

30

MISSION OF MERCY

"WAIT!" TOR LIR SHOUTED AS THE BROWN-AND-white creatures bore down on him, shaking their fists and growling. He could tell they were people, yet they covered their bodies from head to toe in animal skins. A few wore the skin of a bear while others wore that of a panther and other predators of the forest.

Ideally, it was an excellent camouflage for scaring away predators, plus the smell surrounding them would frighten off any beast. They carried sharp sticks more useful for spearing fish than for fighting in the deep. Tor Lir recognized the tools as ones he used to make when he went fishing before he realized the Waters of Nye would give him anything he desired.

Holding his bow and quiver in front of him, he dropped them on the ground as a group of creatures beat Citrine. "We are not your enemies," he declared, hoping the creatures spoke the common tongue.

His eyes slid over to Citrine who was facedown and covered in creatures more than forest. Tor Lir saw blood oozing from her head and legs. He cursed, unhappy her rashness in attacking had led to this cautious predicament. When he looked at the creatures, he sensed their auras of fear and confusion. They wanted to protect their colony, and Tor Lir could tell they did not have malicious intent. Something was threatening them and they were fighting back as they should.

"Tie us up if you must and take our weapons, but I beg of you, let us have a word with your leader before you decide what to do with us. We will help if you will let us."

He was proud of his words—they were ones he'd uttered many times in the forest of Shimla. It was not his true nature to be devious and deceptive, but often some pranks he'd played against other Iaens had landed him in trouble. He recalled being dragged before the queen of the Falidrains to explain why their golden elixir had been stolen. He'd only moved it before the midsummer feast, dared by one of the Jesnidrains, who seemed to be in a constant conflict with the Falidrains.

Tor Lir had once heard a tale of a female Jesnidrain and a female Falidrain who hated each other, and so passed down the hatred between the two species. He'd made the mistake of getting involved and alienated the Falidrains. At least the Jesnidrains still took him in. They were darker than the Falidrains, but just as beautiful with an intoxicating power he was drawn toward.

The Falidrains were lighter and fairer and often seemed overzealous in their pursuit of goodness and peace. Law was their domain, and they followed the law relentlessly by castigating anyone who showed the slightest inclination of disobedience.

Meanwhile, the creatures ceased beating Citrine and shrieked at each other, pointing and making signs with their hands. One of them tossed a rope to the group closest to Tor Lir. Five surrounded him, the sharp points of their spears pointed toward his chest in case he moved.

"Hold out your hands!" one ordered in a guttural voice. The owner of the voice stomped up to Tor Lir, snatching the bow and quiver. The creature then grabbed a length of rope and wound it around Tor Lir's hands until it began to bite into his skin. "Come with us."

Tor Lir nodded. He took a step, and a burlap bag dropped onto his head, shutting out his vision of the forest. It pulled tight against his neck and slowed down his breathing. So much for diplomacy. "Is this necessary?" he demanded.

A stick slammed into his back, a first warning for speaking, and Tor Lir gave up and let them lead him, stumbling, into the forest.

They marched over forested terrain. Tor Lir heard the animals of the wood, voices fraught with fear and panic. Once he heard the throaty trickling of water and remembered Citrine said they should follow a river to find the

Master of the Forest. A sweetness hung in the air, strong enough to get through the burlap on his head. The inside smelled like unwashed feet. He tripped on roots and underbrush and the creatures leading him cursed and rapped him on the head each time he slowed them down.

Eventually, they reached smooth terrain and an arm fell on Tor Lir's shoulder, bringing him to a stop. A furry hand grabbed his wrists and lifted them straight up, tugging until his toes grazed the ground. Tor Lir grimaced as someone yanked the sack off his head, pulling out a few of his black hairs with it. He blinked as his eyes watered, surprised at the sunlight filtering into the place. Tilting back his head, he saw his hands tied above him while a hill sloped down, displaying a strange habitation. A tribe covered in brown-and-white fur surrounded him and Citrine, who was still passed out. Her head hung limply while her arms were tied next to his.

Tor Lir swallowed to gather moisture back into his dry mouth. He took the time to examine his surroundings as he decided what to say. A stream flowed through the middle of the encampment, disappearing into the gray vines of the forest. Thick trees rose on either side, casting cool shadows over the village.

On either side of the stream were huts made out of what looked like sticks for walls and straw for roofs. Ropes and pulleys led up into the trees. Tor Lir saw females and children in the trees, crouched on branches, their faces covered in black paint. They held spears in hand while they peered down at the new prisoners.

Cloth weaved of red-and-white patterns hung from tree branches and lay in front of the doorless opening to huts, like a welcome mat. Sticks for fires were stacked in intervals across the forest village. Baskets of fresh fish, some with their tails wagging in desperation, perched dangerously close to the water as if those fishing had abruptly abandoned their catch.

The people on the ground—mostly males—stood at the bottom of the hill, gazing up at Tor Lir and Citrine. They all appeared around the same height—about five feet—and animal fur covered their lean bodies. Some wore claws on their heads while others had bare arms with runes painted on their bodies. A few of the bolder males sprinted up the hill and gathered around Tor Lir, whispering in their language and poking him with their rather blunt spears.

"Aye, aye." Tor Lir spoke up as he swung, trying to get away from their spears. "Where is your leader?"

The people turned and pointed, saying something like *yah, yah, yah*. They backed away from Tor Lir and Citrine, creating an opening. Tor Lir squinted, yet he saw no one as the tribe's people hummed and chanted, swaying back and forth.

A shadow appeared from within the trees, weaving through the tribe, touching their heads with its black bear claws. It was a head taller than all the people and moved with an intense grace. Tor Lir squinted as the shadow walked into the sunlight and revealed itself as a male.

His aura commanded the fear and respect of his tribe, from the way he walked with his back straight and shoulders tall to the way his dark eyes glittered, examining Tor Lir from head to toe. A scar crossed one of his cheeks as if he'd wrestled with some animal and won, standing out against his tan, dark, leathery skin. His feet were bare because he did not care about the rough terrain of the forest piercing the soles of his feet. He crossed his hands over his chest as he walked up to Tor Lir, gazing at him before turning and spitting into the mud.

"You attacked my people?" The male's bushy eyebrows sank low, his voice deep and ferocious.

Tor Lir stuck his tongue against the roof of his mouth as he determined how to respond. The male gave off an aura difficult to read and Tor Lir was unsure what reaction the words would bring. "Nay. They attacked first. We only defended ourselves."

The male frowned. "You were in our territory."

Tor Lir shrugged as best he could with his hands tied above his head. "There was no warning. If we'd known this was your territory, we would have avoided it."

The male raised a hand and Tor Lir fell silent, recognizing the sign that told him to stop. "The Tribe of Fyn does not welcome strangers. Your arrival is fortunate. You will be the sacrifice for the gods of the forest."

A pulse of adrenaline shot through Tor Lir at the

word *sacrifice*. Memories of the grand sacrifices of blood and fire came to the forefront of his mind, and a sudden nausea rose in his stomach. "It would be to your advantage to let us go. We came to this forest with a purpose and must not be sidetracked, lest a great calamity befall the inhabitants of this wood."

The male's eyes flickered. "A great calamity has befallen this land. You attacked my people and for that, you must pay. A life for a life."

Tor Lir sighed. "My companion"—he jerked his chin toward Citrine—"was overzealous in the use of her knives and for that, I beg forgiveness. We are on a quest and did not intend to interrupt your scavengers. If you will let us go, we will be on our way and will never intrude on your land again."

"Hum . . ." The leader pursed his lips, his brown eyes scanning first Tor Lir and then Citrine. "Does your companion agree?" He pointed at Citrine.

"Er. . . perhaps if she were awake." Tor Lir bit his lip.

"We shall see." He spun, facing his tribe, and ordered, "Prepare the sacrifice!"

Tor Lir's eyebrows shot up. Sacrifices were common enough, and from time to time, he'd joined in the rituals in Shimla, sacrificing a portion of the harvest to the sacred Creator. Most sacrifices involved an altar and burning with fire. Suddenly, he did not feel so cocky. "Perhaps we can come to an agreement? Or trade?"

The male paused before turning to face Tor Lir, his

expression curious. "Trade?" His tone was quiet, commanding respect. "What are you offering?"

"I don't know what you need or want, but you may have our weapons—"

"We already have those," the male interrupted.

Tor Lir realized he was going about it all wrong. He was on the brink of begging for his life instead of bartering. There was a time when he'd stolen jewels from the caves of the Rainidrains. They were not impressed with his apology and teased him until he begged for mercy. At last, tired of their games, he'd grown cold and shouted at them. They scattered, leaving the jewels and tiptoeing around him with respect ever since. He needed to apply the same method in this situation.

Fixing the leader with his eyes, he allowed his expression grow cold and lowered his voice, letting the frosty power drift through him like fingers of ice. "The hospitality of your tribe is lacking. My companion and I are on a quest of mercy. A darkness haunts the lands of Novor Tur-Woodberry, and we seek the Master of the Forest. I assume you have heard of him since you dwell in his domain."

The male's eyes appeared interested, although his face was hard. He blinked once and gave a short nod.

Tor Lir proceeded. "When your tribe attacked us, I tried to speak sense into them and yet they brought us here to be a sacrifice. As their leader, I expect you to lead them with righteousness. It is clear they respect your opinion, and while I offered the weapons in a fair exchange for freedom, I am not so sure your tribe is worth it. I would prefer to discuss before you make any more false accusations against myself and my companion."

"Why are you seeking the Master of the Forest?" The male frowned as he balled his hands into fists.

"To destroy him." Tor Lir let a malicious smile creep into his face, savoring the anticipation of destroying an evil creature.

"Enough." The leader reached behind his back, drew a curved knife, and strode toward Tor Lir.

In one motion, he swept the blade through the air and Tor Lir cringed, waiting for the blow. The knife sang, biting into the rope. His hands fell in front of him.

"If you are going to destroy the Master of the Forest, the Tribe of Fyn will help." The leader placed a hand on his chest.

Tor Lir stopped short of grinning and nodded, thumping his chest twice as he bowed his head to the leader. "My companion and I would be grateful of your assistance."

"I am called Agrim," the leader announced. "Who are you?"

"I have no name, but you may called me Tor Lir. My companion is Citrine." Tor Lir turned toward her. Blood dropped off her face and her bare legs were covered in scratches. "Perhaps you have a healer for her wounds?"

Agrim lifted a hand and snapped twice.

When he finished, a deafening roar shook the forest.

Green leaves dived to the ground in submission, burrowing under weaved baskets and woven cloth. Tor Lir ducked as the heat of wrath surged like an out-of-control fire. As the roar faded, a massive creature burst through the foliage.

31

NEW ENEMIES

AVA, CITRINE'S MIND WHISPERED BEFORE SHE awoke. Her body stung with pain as she opened her eyes, surprised to find her arms tied by her wrists above her head. A roar shook the forest and she peeled her eyes open further, blinking against the sunlight as fury rolled through her. *Ava? Is that you?*

I heard you call and came as soon as I could. What do you want me to do?

These people hurt me. Destroy them and take me away from here.

You know the rule. Never hurt a mortal.

Citrine gritted her teeth at the truth. *Cause chaos then, and set me free.*

Another roar shook the forest, and out of the foliage burst Ava with her blue wings spread. She roared as she flew over the encampment, stretching out her long neck and puffing clouds of white smoke out of her nostrils.

Citrine felt a grim smile come to her lips as she watched her magnificent beast terrify her captors. Ava's massive body flew lower as she waved her long scaly tail back and forth.

People screamed at her appearance, clashing into each other as they dashed for safety. Hammocks collapsed and makeshift tree huts rolled over. Baskets of bright-orange fruit spilled and piles of firewood collapsed as Ava flew, upsetting the caged animals the tribe kept. A rough male voice shouted orders, attempting to bring some semblance of order to the attack and organize a counterattack. Citrine saw a few of the people clothed in animal skins snatch up spears and thrust them at Ava as if mere pointed rocks could pierce her scales. All the same, a fury rose in Citrine and her heart thudded as each spear fell away, harmless.

The spark of mischief blazed in her heart as the people ran. "This is why you don't cross me. Now look who is in your midst! Look who is running now!"

She threw back her head and cackled. The blood ran into her mouth and she almost choked on her own bodily fluids. Ava's warm breath touched her hands as sharp teeth chomped off the rope. Citrine struggled out of her bonds, turning to see where Tor Lir stood free, staring at her in aghast. His face was rather pale, but Citrine was too proud to examine him further. "Tor Lir, with me!" she shouted, grabbing his arm and dragging him toward Ava.

Tossing herself on Ava's back, she pulled Tor Lir up

behind her, scraping her knees against the rough scales. More blood flowed, smarting and stinging while Ava's wide wings beat against the forest floor. *Go. Go. Now!* Citrine encouraged her.

Ava lifted, surging into the air with one final roar.

Take us to the river where Morag dwells.

Are you sure? I don't think you want to go there.

Don't question me—just go.

"Ha, did you see that?" Citrine bragged, using her cloak to wipe blood and gore off her face as she turned behind her to peek at Tor Lir. Both of his arms were around her waist and she assumed he was holding on, fearful of enjoying the pure glory of flying. But when she glimpsed his pallid face, she realized he was gripping her waist with absolute fury.

"How could you?" He spit the words at her. "What have you done?"

Citrine coughed up blood and spit it out over the forest floor as Tor Lir's words sank in. Below she still heard cries from the tribe and the underbrush rustled as they gave chase, following the beating wings of Ava.

"What do you mean what did I do?" she demanded. "I just saved us." She waved her hands in the air, her thighs gripping Ava's back so she would not fall. "And what? You're furious at me for saving us? Because *you* wanted to be the hero?"

"No," he growled back, his grip tightening across her belly, making her gasp. "Don't throw careless words at me. While you were passed out, I was forming an alliance with the Tribe of Fyn and you just destroyed it by attacking them *again*! They were going to help us fight the Master of the Forest. We would have had an army and now we're on our own—*again*—because you're too self-centered to consider the perspective of anyone but yourself. No wonder you're alone with your beasts. The only people who get along with you are the people you can control."

Citrine felt a hot rage sear through her. Something within her snapped and she turned as best as she could, screaming as she balled up her fists and pelted Tor Lir with her hands. "How dare you say such a thing! How dare you! You don't know me at all and yet you judge. I hope you fall and die."

Tor Lir held his hands up, blocking her blows. "See! This is exactly what I mean. You're doing it again. You're the reason people run. You're the reason for the chaos in the land. This is your fault and you won't let anyone help you."

"Be quiet," Citrine shouted, trying to hit him again, but he caught her wrists in his hands, struggling to pin her down. "I hate you," she whispered. "You're the balancer of good and evil, yet all you care about is balance. There are people who need help—"

"People like the Tribe of Fyn," Tor Lir snarled. "Tell your great beast to take us down. I'm done with this adventure and this quest with you, Citrine. You should think about yourself less and consider the greater good.

Perhaps you wouldn't find yourself in quite a predicament."

Citrine closed her eyes as his words rang out and Ava dipped lower, not quite slowing her flight as she moved toward the forest floor. Citrine wanted to drop Tor Lir from the top of the forest, swing down into the leaves, snatch up his broken body, and drop him again. Yet as she sat there, hugging herself and feeling the bruises ache, she realized there was truth to his words. If it weren't for her rashness and anger, they might be in a better predicament.

Ava, take us to the river.

Where did you find this male? Ava snickered. *He's full of words.*

I don't want to talk about it.

Do you want me to toss him from a high cliff? I can kill him for you.

No thanks. Well, maybe after the Master of the Forest is dead. I don't like Tor Lir very much, but I think I need his help.

He's right, you know. The Tribe of Fyn are hunters—they could have helped.

Don't remind me. I'm beaten and I'm tired. I don't want to talk anymore.

MYTHICAL BEINGS

Ava landed near a river where weeping willows perched near the bank. Tor Lir tumbled off the beast, reaching out a hand as he stood back to admire her beauty. Tor Lir felt dwarfed at the monstrous size of the beast yet awed Citrine tamed it. His opinion of her shifted. She was wild and impulsive but with beasts like these on her side, she became dangerous to cross.

After Citrine climbed down, Ava arched her long neck and faced them, tucking her blue wings onto her scaly back. Tor Lir admired the beauty of her colors—blue feathers, green scales blending into the shadows of the forest. Catching the beast's eye, he pressed his hands, palms together, and bowed. "Thank you for your assistance, even though it was unnecessary."

The beast blinked at him and nudged Citrine with her snout. A cloud of smoke rose from her nostrils, invading the air with a warning of fire. Citrine waved the smoke out of her face and stroked the nose of the beast like a lover.

Tor Lir crossed his arms, feeling his spine go rigid at the display of affection between female and beast. "What did she say?" Tor Lir assumed they carried a silent conversation in their minds he could not hear. He scratched his neck, shifting his weight from foot to foot in unease.

"She thinks you're polite, but all the same she laughs at you," Citrine mumbled without looking at him.

Tor Lir sighed. She was still angry with him and her aura was dark red, warning him against trifling with her. He expected short answers would be all he got out of her for now.

Tor Lir wished she would apologize for making a hasty decision without consulting him. Turning his back on the pair, he walked through the mud on the river-bank, recalling a fight he'd gotten into with one of his childhood companions: Nyllen.

Nyllen was the son of a ruler and primed to be king of the Green People, especially when the green giantess —who raised Tor Lir—left. Tor Lir knew Nyllen was jealous of him and they often argued about harmless things until *Gundibage*: Night of the Giving.

It was an annual tradition for the Iaens to remember the night of their rebirth. They remembered their downfall by the eleven Monrages (evil children of Changers) who sought to take ultimate power and rule the Four Worlds. The Iaens celebrated their return to the land

and the rebirth of their kind, provided through the grace of the Creator.

As tradition foretold, they would sacrifice a living creature, and they often selected a Green Person to perform the great honor. Tor Lir and Nyllen fought over the right to lead the sacrifice. It was Tor Lir's responsibility as a ward of the queen, yet Nyllen wanted to take over, since he assumed, correctly, that Tor Lir would not stay around to take the crown. As they argued, Tor Lir realized it did not matter who was right and who was wrong. It took humility to become a leader. He'd been the first to reach out his hand and step down from the position. After that, Nyllen had become a friend and introduced him to the Jesnidrains, who brightened his life with frolics and folly.

"Is this the river you spoke of?" Tor Lir asked Citrine, watching the waters splash across the shallows and slick boulders. The rocks in the river would make the perfect perch for fishing.

"Aye. Ava agrees this is the river. We will follow it for a couple of days until we reach the lair of the Master of the Forest. Ava says she can fly us, but both of us are too heavy. She's still young and hasn't reached her full strength yet."

"It's of no concern." Tor Lir lifted a hand to dismiss her words as he squatted by the riverbank. Cupping his hands, he poured the cool water over his face, refreshing himself from the trek through the woods. "The hour grows late. I dare say we've come far enough for a day.

The sun will soon set and you need to take care of your wounds."

"No thanks to you," Citrine muttered as she strode to the riverbank, placing Ava between herself and Tor Lir.

She took off her cloak, laying it in the mud before adding her shift to it. Tor Lir averted his eyes as she waded into the water and submerged herself, swimming in circles. He'd seen many naked Iaens, shameless as they bathed in the steaming pools known as the Waters of Nye. However, something felt wrong as he let his gaze slip back to Citrine. "Aye," he called. "It is best we hide ourselves before sundown. We don't have weapons, and I expect the forest is less friendly during the night."

"Aye," Citrine quipped, running her fingers through her wet hair. "It's not my fault we don't have weapons."

"It is," Tor Lir disagreed, drying his wet hands on his cloak. "I was about to barter with Agrim, the leader of the Tribe of Fyn, and get them back."

"Oh, will you stop bringing that up! I made a mistake! Okay? Are you happy now?" Citrine shouted, splashing water toward him.

Something within him relaxed, and Tor Lir stood tall, surprised at the apology. "I cannot shake the feeling that we turned potential allies into enemies. I assume they will hunt us down, adding to our woes."

"We know nothing yet," Citrine retorted. She walked out of the water, droplets streaming from her body. She moved for her cloak, wrapping it around herself like a towel. "Back away from the river—he is coming."

"Who?" Tor Lir took a step back in confusion, although his eyes slid over the curves of Citrine's body.

He wondered what it would be like to run his hands over them. She was much bigger and curvaceous than the short and slim Iaens he'd copulated with in Shimla. Tor Lir watched the bruises appear on her body as she pulled on her short frock, and a ripple passed through his lower belly.

An idea came to him and he wondered if there was the possibility of something he'd never considered before. Citrine was right: he did not know much about his powers, and what he did know, he seemed to stumble across by accident. As much as her presence frustrated him, he was curious about what he could do. He held out a hand, watching a glimmer swirl around it as his conscience shut down, focusing on the present. He walked toward Citrine, his hands outstretched.

She jerked back at his proximity, reaching up her hands to pull her wet hair into a braid. Her nostrils flared as she glared at him. "Just because you saw me naked does not give you the right to approach me."

"Nay, I am not lusting after your body," he said, denying the urges of his flesh. "You took quite a beating back there and I might be able to help."

Her eyes narrowed at him, but she stood still, letting her arms fall to her side.

"If you will allow me," he continued, feeling much

like he was taming a wild animal. He'd had his share of taming creatures in the forest, teaching them to curb the desire to bite his fingers off and take food from his hand. He felt the same way as he approached Citrine, his hands out to cup her face. His fingers slid around her neck and he reached his thumbs out to touch her nose as a light danced from his fingers. He felt the soft tissue move under his touch, snapping her broken nose back into place.

Moving his arms down, he caressed her bruised neck. The soft veins were difficult to find, so he did the best he could, lightly touching the bruises, hoping the blood would flow back into place. Placing his hands on her shoulders, he spun her to face the forest. She gasped as his fingertips gingerly touched her raw back. He realized he was humming, a soothing noise, a calm cooing.

Dropping to his knees, he started with her ankles, touching the raw red stripes on the back of her legs, moving up to her thighs while her legs trembled under his touch. He knew the effect he had on the Iaens, but Citrine melted under his touch and he felt something else. A strong desire for power rose up in him, and he lifted his hands higher, barring her smooth buttocks and her back to his tender caress. The stripes on her back were light, but he touched each one all the same before dropping her shift back down. Taking her shoulders, he turned her around to face the waters.

Her breath came short and fast, and her glassy eyes stared at his as her lips parted. She moved toward him, angling her head as he took a step back, knowing what he'd done to her. Before she could utter a word, a bellow came from the river and a wave washed over them, spraying them with a delicate mist from the waters. Tor Lir spun around, his eyes widening at the beast that appeared from the depths.

3 3

MILKY WHITE

CITRINE KNEW SOMETHING WAS WRONG WHEN she saw Morag's eyes. They were white orbs in his massive face. His gray neck reared up out of the waters, thicker than the broad oak trees that spanned the land of Novor Tur-Woodberry. Morag shook his gray snout, water flicking off the two curved horns on his head. Citrine caught her breath as she gazed on his monstrous beauty, thankful for a distraction from the strange allure of Tor Lir. She wanted to break his arms and yet she also wanted to understand his unique abilities. His touch on her body made her shiver and reminded her of pleasures enjoyed in what seemed like a past life.

"Citrine," Morag spoke, his deep voice shaking the weeping willow trees and causing ripples in the water.

Surprise rendered her mute. She expected Morag's voice to resonate in her mind as it did with her other beasts.

211

"We cannot speak in our minds now. We are in the realm of the Master," Morag stated, moving his body toward the shore and fixing his milky-white gaze on Tor Lir. "Who have you brought with you?"

"I don't understand." Citrine glanced at Tor Lir, who stood, wide-eyed, gazing at Morag with an intensity in his emerald eyes. "Why must we speak out loud? Surely the Master of the Forest has spies everywhere and they will hear us?"

"Nay." Morag shook his head, his jagged teeth appearing like a warning in his mouth. "The Master of the Forest is like you. He controls the beasts with his mind, and he has taken me from you. I must do his bidding now. I only returned to tell you, if you don't do something, he will take the lands to the north and south, the east and west. They are falling one by one as we speak, and all the beasts will follow his command."

"Why?" Citrine fought the rising panic in her chest. "Why did you leave me? Why is he taking these lands? Where can I find him?"

"The Master of the Forest is stronger than you. Beware, for he seeks to take all your beasts from you. If you listen, you can hear him speak as I do; he promises a future for the beasts, different from the one you promise. I caution against searching for him. He does not want to see you—he only requests you keep fulfilling your end of the bargain. You have done well thus far."

Citrine could not stop the hot tears that rolled down her cheeks as Morag spoke. His betrayal struck her deep and brought up her own weaknesses. She failed to protect her beasts by giving them a haven. Time ran out while she sought spells and let her beasts roam a forest she knew was evil while she basked in Novor Tur-Woodberry's companionship and enjoyed his land. She failed to take care of Morag, the newest beast in her collection, and he'd left her for someone evil and strong. Perhaps that was why she had not heard from Zaul; he had also switched to a new master with a different promise. The threads of control slipped from her fingers, one by one. Would she lose everything she cared about?

"What did he promise you?" Citrine demanded as Morag sank down, his shadow disappearing from the mud while his ruined eyes glazed over like clouds over the sunlight.

"I cannot disobey the Master. To speak of his wishes is to encourage death."

"Morag, wait!" Citrine ran to the edge of the bank, her heart thudding in her chest as she watched the water beast sink below the waves. "Don't give up. I will save you this time. You'll see."

Morag paused before his head disappeared underwater while waves nipped at his nostrils. He opened his mouth, a row of sharp teeth appearing, his voice louder and deeper as the acoustics of the wave took on his tone. "The Master of the Forest is old and resolute—leave while you can, before he takes you too."

"Citrine." Tor Lir's hand touched her shoulder. She

slapped it away, furious at displaying weakness in front of him. "Let him go. We will come up with a plan."

Ava lifted her head from where she perched by the waters, watching the exchange out of lidded eyes. *I can kill Morag for you.*

Before Citrine could answer, another voice came through her thoughts and she reeled in surprise. *Did you see? Did you see what I can do? Did you see your beasts turn on you?*

Citrine ran to Ava and threw her arms around the beast's neck, fear coursing through her body. Her limbs shook as she hung on tight, leaning her cheek against Ava's solid feathers. She stood still, taking steadied breaths as she regained her strength and determination. *Air of clarity. Help me do the right thing this time.* At last, pulling back, she placed her hands on Ava's snout, forcing the beast to look her in the eye. Ava's eyes were still a pure citrine, and she blinked lazily as she let out a low growl. "Don't speak, Ava. Run!" Citrine said. "If you can, find Grift and Zaul, but don't worry too much about them. Get out of the forest. Go where the Master of the Forest can't reach you. I won't risk losing you."

You won't lose me.

"Don't speak. Just go before something happens."

Leaning forward, she planted a kiss on Ava's nose and let go, glaring at Ava until the beast spread her wings, almost knocking Citrine over. Ava's great claws left giant prints in the mud by the riverbank as she took off, spreading her wings wide as she coasted with the warm evening air.

Citrine put her hands on her hips and turned to find Tor Lir. He sat on the bank, his hands on his knees and his eyes closed as if he were sleeping. "Tor Lir, are you coming?" She let the words drop from her lips as hard as sharp stones.

He lifted his head and opened his eyes, pressing his hands into the ground. "Where are you going?"

"You heard Morag. There is no time for sleep. I have to find the Master of the Forest and take back my beasts."

Tor Lir glanced at the water and nodded. "This is personal for you now, but we can't march into the lair of this creature without a plan."

Citrine scowled hard. She was used to being spontaneous with her decisions. "If you want a plan, think on it while we walk." A pang of remorse swept through her as she wished she had her pack of herbs and knives. A dull gnaw of hunger poked at her belly and she wrapped her arms around her abdomen, recalling the touch of Tor Lir's gentle fingers. Most males had rough hands from hard work and calluses on their fingers.

He nodded once as he rose and walked toward her. She spun, finding her way along the shore, picking smooth rocks out of the mud as she did so. Tor Lir was silent behind her, and part of her wished he would speak while another part of her wished the night would swallow him up.

Darkness came swiftly with cruel fingers while yellow eyes glittered into the darkness. The cry of animals ripping each other apart in the underbrush made Citrine hug close to the shore, frustrated with her lack of weapons. She fingered the stones she slipped in her pockets, hoping she'd be able to craft a crude slingshot. Hunger disappeared as she listened to the ferocious nocturnal animals while white seeds lit up the river, eerie in the dim, moonless night.

A luminous glow appeared near the riverbed. Citrine squinted as she and Tor Lir neared a patch of land where florescent mushrooms lit up the darkness. Deep blues and light pinks poured off the mushrooms like mist, the colors flowing into the water where they disappeared with a poof while fireflies winked in and out of view. Citrine paused, tempted to remove her boots and bury her bare feet in the mud, letting the fungi grow around her toes. She wanted to taste the colors dancing through the air and take their secrets as her own. Suddenly, she understood Grift's strong desire to eat everything and discover secrets for himself.

A fierce cry echoed from the woods. Citrine balled her hands into fists as the memory of a fight with a panther flickered into her perturbed thoughts. She saw a flash of white and felt her body grow cold as the waif who'd given her the skull peered out from behind a tree.

34

FLASHES OF WHITE

"WHAT ARE YOU DOING HERE?" CITRINE'S sharp tongue rang out.

Tor Lir jerked his head up. He had been staring at the strange mushrooms. They reminded him of something and a cold discomfort filled him because it was something he did not want to remember. Perhaps it wasn't memory, only a knowing he did not want to unlock. He watched the pinks and blues morph together, spinning into words he did not want to read. Citrine's sudden interruption was a welcome distraction. He opened his mouth to answer when he saw her march toward something white standing in the trees. The creature peeked around a tree trunk, her strands of hair silver in the dim light.

"It's you!" Tor Lir exclaimed, surprised to see the bone-white creature who'd led him out of the forest.

"Are you following me?" Citrine demanded.

Tor Lir watched her take an aggressive step toward the creature and hurried to her side, reaching to grab her elbow. "Citrine, it's all right. She will not harm us."

Citrine spun, snatching her elbow out of his hand, uttering a low growl in her throat. "Do you know her?"

Tor Lir nodded, watching Citrine's expression change from surprise to disbelief. "Aye. Do you recall? I told you I met a creature in the wood."

"You met *her*?" Citrine's words came out like a snarl. "She's with the Master of the Forest. Why didn't you say so!"

Tor Lir paused, rearranging his thoughts. "How do you know her?"

"The skull," Citrine whispered.

Tor Lir took a step, but Citrine's hand slammed into his chest, pushing him away. The bone-white creature held a finger to her thin lips, shaking her head. Dismissing her warning, Tor Lir crept toward her, holding out a hand and beckoning. "Please, don't be afraid. Speak to me," he begged, a rush of curiosity propelling him forward.

The creature stalked out from behind the tree, her slender body waving back and forth. Her dark eyes were wide as she glared at him. "I told you not to come back." She sounded angry as she raised her hand and pointed a bony finger at his chest. "I gave you mercy once, but now you shall have none. You've entered the realm of the Master, and there is no escape."

"What did you do?" Citrine demanded, her hot

218

breath at his shoulder. Spittle touched his neck, and he wiped it away, sandwiched between two angry females. "You took my memories and forced me to bury the skull," Citrine said and Tor Lir realized she was talking to the bone-white creature. He tilted his head and studied her out of the corner of his eye. Her vibrant hair stood out in the darkness as if it carried its own light and shadows.

"I do as the Master instructs," the creature snapped, her voice cold.

"Will you take us to the Master?" Tor Lir dropped his hand on the creature's shoulder.

Her expression changed and her eyes became wide with liquid. Her voice dropped to a whisper. "The Master does not want to see you. If I take you to him, he will take you too and the voices will never leave you alone. You will do his bidding, and his desires will become your desires."

Tor Lir gripped her shoulder harder. "Is he speaking to you now?"

"You're interrupting." She pulled away. "Go now, before it is too late."

The creature turned and walked away, weaving between the trees.

"Follow her," Citrine hissed as she poked him in the ribs. She moved off at a run, trailing the creature.

A vibration rushed through Tor Lir, heavy with the knowledge he needed to fix the balance. All the pieces were there and he knew with certainty he just needed to put them together. He paused on the shore, torn between going back for Agrim's army he knew would be useful. However, Citrine and the bone-white creature had the key to finding the Master, and he was unsure he could find the river again in such a strange forest. Glancing back, the odd lights from the mushroom confirmed his choice. Lifting his feet, he ran after Citrine.

The aura of the forest held a creeping sensation of evil, a glaring difference from the sensuous enchantments of Shimla. He ran from the words of light the mushrooms would imprint on his brain. They haunted him as if he'd said them out loud repeatedly. *If you want to know who you are and where you came from, go to Daygone.*

He wagged his head from side to side, wishing words would fall out of his ears so he could trample them on the ground. *Knowledge. Wealth. Power. Could all be yours if you read the book of your people. Long may you live. Long may you prosper.*

His hands flew to his head, and he pressed against his ears, willing to make the words cease. An aura of potent darkness surrounded the words. He did not want to know. If he found out the knowledge, he would lose his soul, and he was too young. He did not desire to dwell with darkness. He had so much to live for, so much to explore.

Lost in his thoughts, he was surprised when moisture surrounded him. He lifted his hands and noticed the fine dew that heralded the morning coming down on his head. The forest was lighter and the ghastly noises of night all but consumed by the hope of daytime. He saw Citrine bend over by a tree, her hand on the trunk as she caught her breath. Sweat covered her body and as he caught up, he saw her eyes were glazed over and red-rimmed from lack of sleep.

"You should rest," he whispered.

She stood tall, throwing back her shoulders before her eyes widened and she pointed. Tor Lir followed her fingers and froze as a coldness swept over him. Flashes of white surrounded them. The bone creatures were coming, and they did not look friendly.

35

REALM OF BEASTS

A DRUM ECHOED IN CITRINE'S MIND. SHE stared at the bone-white creatures marching down the hillside toward her and Tor Lir. Some gripped bones in their hands, held up like clubs. Others carried drums made of skin pulled taut over hollow bone. They had tied the drums about their waists and beat on them with short dark bones.

Dum. Da dum. Dum. Da dum.

When she glanced behind, she saw them circling around and flashbacks whipped through her mind.

Crawling through a tunnel. Darkness. Gray vines reaching out like fingers, snatching at her hair and tugging her forward. The skull in her hand, the horns growing longer and sharper like the fine point of a needle. Setting it in a nested throne deep belowground. A beast carrying and then dropping her. Waking during daylight.

Memories returned to her, but it was the voices that flooded her mind.

Beat the drums. Beat them. Don't let them stop.

Take them to the Master. Move.

Flesh becomes bone. Bone becomes flesh.

Save me from the monsters. Save me. Save me.

Beat the drums.

Move.

Save me. Save me.

Bone becomes flesh.

Beat the drums.

Save me.

Flesh becomes bone.

The Master calls.

Move.

The words filtered through her mind like hundreds of voices speaking, feeling, thinking all at once. She sensed emotions, fearful and angry, obedient yet longing for release. A tidal wave roared through her mind and as she watched, opening her eyes wider to take it in, darkness consumed her vision. She held out her hands, her fingers snatching for support. Something reached her, its arms sliding around her waist. When she put a hand down, she felt the sickly skinny bone and fainted.

Citrine opened her eyes to darkness. As her vision adjusted, she saw a shadowy kingdom, with gray vines growing along interlocking trees. The bark was black with sap and a bitter sweetness hung in the air mixed with a hint of sulfur and the disgust of decay. Citrine shifted, surprised she stood upright, but when she flexed her fingers, rope dug into her wrists. Glancing down, she found they had tied another rope around her waist, binding her to a tree. Sap dripped onto her fingers and she realized while she was passed out, it had coated and crusted on her hands.

The voices that had been in her head were silent and while she wanted to reach out feelers of communication for her beasts, she didn't want the multitude of voices to return. It must be how the Master controlled them—he held their minds hostage. It was a vengeful act and something Citrine wondered if she could do with her beasts. Nay, it was violent and evil to take free will away from any living creature. A desire to vomit rose in her belly and she swallowed hard, fighting to keep it down.

Distracting herself, she looked around. Before her was what appeared to be a throne carved into a towering redwood tree. Telltale signs of death gathered on its trunk while gray vines and black branches curved toward the sky, creating the seat and back to the wide throne. At the base of the throne, she saw something moving back and forth and as she squinted in the darkness, she saw black-and-red snakes slithering on the ground as if creating steps for the owner of the throne to walk upon.

Hanging from the branches above the throne were different bones: a jaw with bloody teeth in it, the skeletal fingers of a hand, a skull, smaller without teeth, and several feet. Bones littered the ground right up to her feet, several gnashed and broken as if some great beast with teeth gnawed on them.

A terrifying realization came over Citrine as a creature moved out of the shadows. He had limbs like branches of a tree grown out of dark wood. Black ivy crawled around his limbs, as if holding them together, while a cloak of blood-dusted feathers swirled around him.

His face appeared to be the skull of a strange animal, a cross between a deer and something bigger and broader. Bone-white covered the creature's face and yet its bones were rotted to the core, giving off the distasteful odor of sulfur and decay. A crown of antlers at least a foot tall rose from its head. The black slots for eyes regarded her with a chilling menace.

The Master walked on the snakes that froze as his feet squashed their bodies. The snakes resumed their movement, some jerking back and forth in pain as the Master turned his antlers and interlocked them into the branches of the throne. He sat down and waved his three-fingered, clawed hand at Citrine, his words whispering through the stillness.

"Enchantress."

Citrine fought against her fears as the creature spoke her name and the bite of revulsion made her shiver. She was well aware of her situation and licked her dry lips as she decided what to say. If she called her beasts to save her, the Master would take them. It was best to determine what he wanted with her. In her first meeting with him, he'd shown no animosity—only asked her to be the agent of chaos.

"We meet again," the Master of the Forest continued, his voice low and sultry. "I did not expect to find you in my forest again, not after our agreement some months ago. Yet here you are with heightened powers, which is curious and fortunate for me. I think you belong in my world."

Citrine spoke once she got her feelings under control. "I don't think so." This time she would control her temper. "Why am I tied up? As you said, we had an agreement. Are you changing the terms?"

The Master's snout curved up in what Citrine assumed was a wicked smile but appeared more like a grimace. "Do not take me for a fool. You went to Paradise and fell in love with its charms and then came here to shatter the realm of beasts by taking my forest and my beasts from me. My beasts determined you would harm them or myself, and I instructed them to tie you up so we might speak to clear the air between us."

Citrine narrowed her eyes, frustrated the Master of the Forest saw through her plans. For a moment, she regretted distracting Tor Lir's parley with the Tribe of Fyn. She should have listened to him and entered the realm prepared to fight. She eyed the glade, yet it seemed it was just her and the Master. The bone-white beasts and Tor Lir must be elsewhere.

"You have a flair for misdeeds and mischief. If you join my revolution, you may have safety for all your beasts and the Paradise you so desire. Why do you care about the mortals? Especially after what they did to you, your herb garden, and your beasts. They never cared for your gifts."

Citrine felt something tear within her. How did the Master of the Forest know about her past life? Who had spoken to him about it? "Nor do you except for personal gain," she snapped, furious at the knowledge he held concerning her past life in the village.

"Personal?" The Master of the Forest tilted his head as he considered the word. "You think this is personal? Nay. The forest is my domain and the dead have woken. They are weary from life and need flesh to cover their bones. Once they are clothed, they may walk upon the ground and mingle with mortals."

Citrine glowered. "They already walk upon the ground with their sickly bones."

"Flesh is what's needed to complete the change." The Master lifted his clawed hands and clicked them together. "Then they will feel life enter their bodies and they will live a second life, a transformed life with a new chance."

"To what end?" Citrine muttered, yet still curious about the Master's plan.

The Master rested his arms on the throne, his claws still tapping against the wood. "In the days of the war, life was not precious and priceless. The Black Steeds—

those who made their alliance with the Monrages and Changers—destroyed all without a thought for life. The people groups fell and their numbers became scarce. In order for the Four Worlds to continue, there must be an abundance of life, and I will give life back to the land. Many of the lost souls became stranded in the afterlife, and I am giving them a chance to remedy their ways. Given the opportunity, would you want to change your destiny and give yourself the chance to enter Paradise?"

A horror gripped Citrine and twisted her heart, and yet she could not deny the curiosity that glowed there. What would it be like to be a lost soul called back from the Beyond to live a second life? "I would agree with you, but calling the dead back to life is drastic. They are dead. Their spirits should rest."

"Nay. It is the cycle of reincarnation. The dead come back to life and are given a second chance to live again. Wouldn't you like the chance to live again with a clean slate? Mistakes of the past gone? A chance to get your life right this time?"

"It sounds exhausting," Citrine murmured. "I don't want to die and I don't know if I want to live forever."

"When you lie on your death bed, you will realize you should have taken my offer. I will not call your spirit back into the world. I will let your bones rot and sink into the ground to renew the plants of the forest. They are old and dying. New life must grow from here."

"What will you do when the undead regain flesh?"

"Fill the land with them. All other secrets are mine.

If you become my mistress and rule in this realm of beasts, all knowledge could be yours."

Citrine shuddered at the word *mistress*, yet she recognized the chance she had there. The Master did not mean to kill her. "Answer me this. Why did you invade the land of Novor Tur-Woodberry?"

"He is powerful, and with the power in his land the undead will have flesh again and live like mortals."

"When you complete your conquest, will it leave anything of the land? Will any of the people be left? Will there be any power for Paradise to grow again?"

"No. You do not understand. Paradise must die so that many will live. It is for the greater good."

"It is for chaos and evil. You must find another way!"

"There is no other way. Either you join me, or I will end you and take your beasts."

"You will take my beasts?" Citrine gritted her teeth as rage flowed through her. Again Morag's filmy white eyes flashed in her memory and hot fury surged through her brain. "Is that why you know so much about me? You've been planning to steal my beasts and use them against me? Is that what you did to Morag?"

"I am like you. You left your mind open and now I can read it. I can see your past, your present, and your desires. You forgot to keep your guard up. My offer tempts you and you are afraid to die. But if you will not join me as my mistress, I will take your flesh."

The Master of the Forest freed his antlers from the

crown and strode down the steps of his throne. Crossing the clearing toward Citrine, he lifted a clawed hand.

Citrine drew back, pressing her head against the hardened sap on the tree, her eyes growing wide as a claw touched her face and then stroked her cheek. It felt like the lightest scratch moving over her skin, something she wanted to press harder into until it drew blood. Torn by her dark desires, she moved her head away in anger. The unexpected slap of the Master's bony hand against her cheek made her eyes water. Her head jerked back and slammed into the tree. A dull pain thudded in her skull.

Citrine turned her furious eyes on the Master, speaking through gritted teeth. "You did not give me a chance to respond."

"You responded. I heard your thoughts. Part of you is enticed by this darkness but deep down inside, you want to *be* the Master. You want to kill me."

"You took the thing most precious and dear to me." She spit her words at him. "My beasts."

The Master of the Forest gave a deep chuckle, his voice echoing through the trees. "I told you when we first met. If you want your beasts, you must fight for them."

As if he'd called them, bone-white faces peeked from behind trees and crept toward them on all fours, jumping through the thicket like animals. "I took more than your beasts. Who do you think drove you out of your home and turned the villagers against you? You aren't the only one who can plant the seeds of chaos."

Citrine blinked hard as the realization hit her like a punch to the stomach. She felt the bottom drop out of everything she'd known and tears started in her eyes. Bile rose in her throat, but there was nothing in her stomach. She gasped, dry heaving as the ropes held her fast. "You monster! You wanted this to happen. You ruined my life!"

"Nay, I gave you the chance to live again. I gave you a gift, but your thoughts give you away. We made a deal. I assumed you would respect that. Seems I was wrong about you." His hand came up, and the claws curled around her neck, the sharp ends ready to peel flesh from bone.

"Let me go," she said through gritted teeth. "I will never be your mistress. You are the destroyer!"

"I am the Master of the Forest." The Master chuckled again as his claws squeezed tighter.

Although her hands were bound, she lifted her leg to knee him in the groin. Her kneecap hit hard bone and her eyes flashed as pain surged through her leg. The Master laughed, delighting in her fury.

"Just for revenge, just so you will never cross me again, I shall destroy Paradise." The Master of the Forest released her throat and pointed claws at her neck, daring her to speak or move lest he rip her in half. "Beasts of the forest," the Master of the Forest shouted. "Go to Paradise. Slay all mortals and take up your new flesh!"

36

THE BONE TREE

AN UNDERCURRENT OF DREAD HUNG IN THE air as Novor Tur-Woodberry strode through the land. Gray clouds drifted through the sky, not because of the need for rain. No, these clouds were a harbinger of impending doom.

He walked past the cottage where Citrine lived. It looked lonely perched on the hill by itself. No smoke curled from the chimney and the door stood wide open as if she'd left in a hurry and forgot to shut it.

The Singing Men built the cottage years ago for the first family who intended to live in the land. The call of adventure bade them leave after just a few months and after that, Novor Tur-Woodberry decided newcomers would live in the village where the green hills rolled endlessly and the breathtaking view inspired joy. The Mouth of Heaven.

The village sat just above the Silver-White Heart,

which breathed life into the land. As long as it was pure, Paradise would flourish. Earlier Novor Tur-Woodberry had gone to see the pulsing orb of light, and darkness poured out of its core.

Frowning at the memory, Novor Tur-Woodberry continued past the cottage and a Trespiral materialized with a shimmer. A young face peering through wide eyes as Novor Tur-Woodberry approached its tree. "Novor Tur-Woodberry, you've come at last." She bowed her head, bringing her branches together with respect.

"You've been expecting me?" He crossed his arms, concerned she hadn't called for his help.

"I'm afraid." She cast her eyes down. "The tree is growing. The ravens flee and the woodland creatures are moving."

"Because of the roots," Novor Tur-Woodberry finished. He'd heard muttering about the roots being too strong. The creatures must be complaining about the white tree. "Who else have you told about the tree?"

"I haven't seen it. I'm only telling you what the ravens told me." The spirit of the tree swayed. "It is coming for my roots. I must hibernate before it takes over."

Novor Tur-Woodberry frowned. As much as he wanted to reassure the tree, his words would not ring true. He walked away, for he knew what he had to do. Earlier that morning, he'd told his Singing Men to go to the Mouth of Heaven and escort the villagers to his home. Given the speed of mere mortals, even if the wild horses assisted, it would take them the better part of the day to move into his home. It was his last defense against the coming darkness.

Walking down the hill, he moved to the middle of the land where a dirty white object glimmered in the light. The gray clouds covered the sun and only the Green Light hung in the sky, a glow of emerald displaying his path. The once green grass underneath his feet lay like chewed cud, chomped to bits and then spit out. Worthless.

He sniffed. A dry rot hung in the air with faint hints of decay. It grew as he approached the tree. It was the color of bone, a dirty white with dead limbs that reached out like skeletal fingers. Its branches pointed in all directions and it appeared like a giant, spiky bush. Charred black grass surrounded the tree as if it were burnt with an intense fire. The tree moved.

Novor Tur-Woodberry's eyes narrowed. The tree moved again. Creatures formed on its branches, budding like flowers but growing at a rapid pace. Novor Tur-Woodberry took a step back, the height of his power ebbing like a dammed river. The largest creature swung on a branch, a head and eyes appearing as it noticed Novor Tur-Woodberry. The thing twisted, snapping the top of its head off the tree, and leaped down, its feet striking the grass with a soft smack.

"Go back!" Novor Tur-Woodberry roared. "You are on my land and must adhere to my laws. Go back to the darkness from whence you have sprung!"

Dark hollows for eyes turned to Novor Tur-Woodberry's face as the creature hunched on all fours, grinding its teeth. It opened its mouth and words snaked out as if the creature were poisoning the land with its words. "The barrier is down. The Master controls this land now, and it is *you* who are trespassing. Do you know what happens to trespassers?"

Novor Tur-Woodberry took another step back, frowning. He knew what the beast would do and watched as one by one, an army of bone-white creatures sprung from the tree.

AGRIM'S ARMY

Tor Lir ran through the forest alone and unhindered. After Citrine fainted, the bone creatures had swooped her up and run off. They ignored his shouts as if he wasn't there, although the female creature gazed at him. Her eyes were wide with sorrow and relief.

Tor Lir felt a swelling in his chest as he ran, but his feet came to a stop when tall reeds rose in his path. He'd have to weave through them, creating a path for himself, but it wasn't just the reeds that stopped him. There was a knowing, deep in his heart. He held his hands palm down as he knelt in front of the reeds and placed his hands on the mud.

A slight tremor shook the ground. Folding his body in half, he placed his ear against the cool dirt. A rumble in the distance sounded, and he closed his eyes, letting his thoughts swirl as he weighed the pros and cons of his actions. If he ran to the lair of the Master, he risked being caught. He needed a weapon and a way to beat the Master at his game. Tor Lir understood the balance was off because of both Novor Tur-Woodberry and the Master.

The thudding grew in intensity and Tor Lir rose, moving into the reeds to observe what came his way. As he peered out with narrowed eyes, he saw a group of black panthers leap through the trees and pad up and down the riverbank. The panthers were giant beasts, standing as high as a male's waist. On their backs were the fur-covered people of the Tribe of Fyn.

A slight smile came to Tor Lir's lips, and he stepped out of his hiding place as the leader, Agrim, spun a panther toward him. Agrim hefted a spear in one hand and pointed it toward Tor Lir's neck. "Where did the beast go?" he demanded, his scarred face twisting in a snarl.

Tor Lir held up his hands. "I mean you no harm. The beast has flown, and they have captured the female."

The snarl left Agrim's face, and he lowered his spear, waving a hand for the warriors behind him to lower their weapons. Resting a hand on the panther's head, Agrim stroked it until it stopped growling and relaxed. "Who was she captured by? How come you are standing here? Free?"

"The white creatures made of bone. Do you know about them?"

"Aye, as we spoke before, they come and take what

they desire, leaving death behind. They have been raiding my tribe for days, despite the barrier we built against them. They are swift and move into darkness, here and gone in a flash. Like lightning."

"I believe I know where they came from, and I intend to stop them, but I need help."

Agrim grunted. "I am listening."

Tor Lir pointed to the river. "The Master of the Forest is taking the beasts and controlling them. I believe if we follow the river, we shall reach his lair."

Agrim frowned. "To what end? To submit to the control of the Master? How will you stop him?"

Tor Lir let the emotion slide out of his face. He gazed into Agrim's dark eyes as he let the ice cold invade through his body. A hostile aura surrounded him and he spoke firmly. "You don't know who I am. Some call me Tor Lir, but I am the Nameless One. I came to keep the balance between good and evil. The Master of the Forest has invoked my wrath, and I go to his lair to set things right. I need you and your warriors to come with me, but choose. I will not beg you. I will only accept your offer freely given."

Agrim scowled and placed a hand on his thigh. "What of the beasts that terrify my tribe?"

"I cannot guarantee peace—this forest is full of mischief. I sense the chaos in each step I take."

"I do not ask for peace, only the demise of those unnatural beings that flood this forest with malice."

"Then come with me."

Agrim swung a leg over the panther's side and leaped to the ground. His fur covered him like a camouflage as he turned back to the tribe. One by one, they lifted their hands, made a fist, and thumped their chests. Agrim placed a hand over his chest and bowed to them. Walking to the male on his left, he held out a hand. The male handed him a bow and quiver that Tor Lir recognized as the weapons Novor Tur-Woodberry had given him.

"You will need these." Agrim tossed them to Tor Lir.

Catching the weapons, Tor Lir slung the quiver onto his back and let the coolness of his aura drift as he met Agrim's eyes. He nodded back at the male. "I had a feeling about you and your tribe. A good feeling."

Agrim mounted the panther. "I harbor no animosity between you and me, but your friend, the female, she will have to answer to what her beast did."

Tor Lir nodded, accepting the words. There must be a remedy for what Citrine and her beast did to the tribe's home.

"You need a mount," Agrim added.

Tor Lir gave him a wry grin. "Follow me. Silence is of the essence from here."

CONTROL

A MEMORY OF YELLOW LIGHT AND A BASKET full of green herbs took Citrine back to her childhood. She recalled her mother taking the herbs out of the basket and placing them on a long board in the sunshine. She hummed a tune and pointed to each herb. "What is this called? Do you remember?"

"Lavender?" Citrine asked. "Thyme. Rosemary. Mint. Sage. Ginseng." She grew more confident in her knowledge as she continued down the line of herbs. "Rose hips."

Mother nodded, her vibrant hair changing colors in the sunlight. Orange. Yellow. Silver. White. "Now that you know their names and how to recognize them in the wild, you must learn how to use them for your benefit. Understand?"

Citrine shrugged in confusion. "Why do we study the herbs? No one else does."

"Ah, but you are mistaken. The Healers have always used herbs to help relieve maladies among the people groups and animals."

"But we are not Healers," Citrine pointed out.

Mother shook her head and picked up a bunch of lavender, the purple blossoms still wide open. "Nay, all the same, you must know the herbs. My favorite is lavender for the air of clarity combined with ginseng. If you need to clear the mind and calm your thoughts, a pinch of these herbs will help. Do you hear the voices yet?"

"Sometimes when I'm by the pond, the frogs speak to me."

"Out loud or in your head?"

"I can hear them in my head. The butterflies whisper, and the dragonflies hum a song without words."

"Be careful with the voices, my little enchantress. You may speak to them, but never force them to do anything. You must not exert your control over the beasts. They are free animals; although some may swear servitude to you, remember, you must always let them have free will. What is the rule we have?"

Citrine swallowed hard and looked down. "I don't remember."

A hand came out, slapping her cheek. "You must remember. Never forget. Now say it with me: *never harm another.*"

"Never harm another." She'd bitten back the tears at the slap, aware she needed to learn and understand. She was too young to notice the double standard her parents had. They pushed her hard and punished her for forgetting and making mistakes.

"Good. Now these herbs will help you if the voices become too much. I'll show you my recipe, but you must keep it a secret . . ."

The memory faded away and Citrine's eyes flew open. It was silent in the glade. Her throat was sore from thirst and her arms ached from being pulled tight behind her back. Three spots of blood had dripped and then dried on her throat from where the Master's claws scraped her. The sickly sweetness of sap made her head hurt, while the throne before her was empty. She closed her eyes again, shutting out the present and stilling herself as she searched.

When she was young, the world was vibrant with sound. She'd heard many voices and as she grew older, she filtered them out and protected her mind from the continual words dancing around her. Youth and innocence quickly evaporated, and she'd been excited to strike out on her own. She'd left her parents, who she assumed still lived close to the fortress in the east. They were loners, hiding their unusual gifts from the people groups, and yet Citrine thought she could find them again if she opened the connection of communication that led back to them. However, her need for them was gone and although she'd never disobeyed the instructions they gave her, control sounded promising.

Shifting her weight from foot to foot, she ignored the itching on her head. Taking a deep breath, she felt the thread of communication and stilled herself for the influx of thought. She opened the doors and a wave of voices rushed in.

Citrine had only been to Oceantic once. Father took her after a bad spell when the voices overwhelmed her and made her nose bleed. Each morning she'd wake, blood pouring from her nose as the voices screamed inside, too many to distinguish what they said. Finally, Father took her on a two-day journey to the white shores where endless waves lapped against the sand. They sat there watching until dark clouds rolled over the horizon and the wind blew strong around them. Sand lifted off the beach and rolled into mini cyclones, and Citrine held Father's hand, watching with interest and wondering if they should seek safety.

"The waves rise high now. See." Father pointed. "They will come rolling in with a magnitude of strength and sweep us away if we lose our footing."

"But we won't lose our footing if we don't go in." Citrine looked up into her father's calm face, but his citrine eyes never left the water.

"We are going in. The waves are like the voices. You

must learn to navigate them if you are to control them. Once you learn, the nosebleeds will stop."

Citrine squeezed Father's hand as fear swirled through her. "I am afraid. I don't want to go in."

"You must not be afraid." Father's tone was firm. "Fear will always try to stop you, but you must act, regardless of the fear. Be brave. Step out."

Citrine stood still, watching the wind whip up and the waves rise higher. "How will standing in the waves help me control the voices?"

"It always helps to navigate the physical world before delving into the complex themes of the intangible world. I will be with you—this time. But you must take the initiative to step out."

Citrine had let go of Father's hand and stepped into the waves. When she closed her eyes, the storm roared around her, but when she found a rock and anchored herself to it, she found she could withstand the wind and waves. It was difficult. She'd slipped, been submerged and coughed up more water than ever before. But she survived, and that was enough.

Now the voices blasted through her mind, making her eardrums ring, and a slow trickle came to her nose.

First, she heard the voices of trees giving into the death grip of the gray vines. Mentally, she closed that door and put out her feelers for more. Creatures thrashed in the forest and drank from the river, bickering with sullen voices. She pulled her feelers away from them.

Searching, she found Ava, flying high above the forest, and Morag, sulking in the bottom of the river, feeling lower than the bottom feeders that scuttled along the mud. Her heart went out to him and she saw the foggy threads of control surrounding him. Moving down inch by inch, she reached out to him, plucking back the strings of control, one by one, hoping the Master was too distracted to notice. She felt Morag's senses awake as the spell of control lifted from him. *Don't speak. Just run*, she told him, heart pounding.

A drop of blood fell onto her lip, begging to be wiped away. She twisted her bound hands, but the rope held firm and she dived in again, sending her feelers of communication onward. Now and then, she came up hard and fast against something that she assumed were other mortals. Animals were her gifting; she'd never had the ability to communicate with mortals in her mind.

As the minutes dragged by, she became uneasy. What if the Master was hiding his mind in the same way— what if she couldn't read it? Although she assumed if he could read her mind, she could read his, unless his power was much greater. Anger surged through her at the thought of Paradise being taken by the bone-white creatures, and she clenched her sap-crusted fingers as she dug deeper.

Blood ran from her other nostril, and she opened her

mouth to breathe through it. A thudding began in her head and a throbbing pain began at the base of her skull. Ignoring the physical discomfort, just like she had in the storm, she dug through layers of communication, opening her feelers and closing them. She found Grift. The strands of control had barely begun, but she pulled them free and sent him the same message. *Don't speak. Just run.*

Digging deeper, she found Zaul, the spark of communication almost gone with a grip so strong she did not know where to begin. There was nothing for it; unless she destroyed the Master, she could not set him free. Squeezing her eyes tighter, she gave it all she had while blood ran over her mouth and dripped down her chin. There. She'd found it. The mind of the Master. It was open and churning with an array of dark thoughts. Reaching through all the threads of communication she'd closed, she opened them and channeled them to the Master, sending a tidal wave of conflicting voices into his mind.

39

LAIR OF THE MASTER

A ROAR OF FURY BELLOWED OUT OF THE WOOD and Tor Lir paused, crouching down in the thicket. "We are here," he whispered to Agrim. "Now, I will go in, face the Master, and find Citrine. On my signal. Attack."

"As discussed," Agrim grunted.

His tribe hid in the thick underbrush. They'd had to dismount and move on foot while their panthers slinked through the forest. Some males had scaled trees and were making hand signals to each other.

Tor Lir crept into the darkness, twisted ivy growing up each tree, choking out their existence and hiding the light. A distinct smell of sulfur hung in the air and as Tor Lir approached, he saw a dark throne made of wood and ivy dripping with sap. A creature made of bone knelt before it. It had three claws for fingers and each clawed hand gripped the side of its head as it knelt, facing away from the throne and howling. It had a long snout like a crocodile and a crown of antlers curved up from its head. Long bones made up its limbs and although it roared in fury, a creeping sensation of angst came over Tor Lir. He swallowed hard, wanting nothing more than to back away. Hollow words twisted through his memory. A cloud of darkness. A green shimmer. A knowledge forced on him when he did not want it. Dread sat heavy on his heart because he wanted to understand and yet he wanted to flee lest the darkness enter and corrupt him.

Forcing himself to move, he took a tentative step, trying to see what the creature was facing. Something white darted out of the woods and sprang in front of him, snarling. As the thing reached for him, another flash of white appeared and bowled it over. The bone-white creature stood before him, her limbs shaking and her eyes cast down.

Tor Lir glanced from her to the creature lying head-long in the ground. "What are you doing here?" he asked.

"My allegiance was to the Master, but the bonds are breaking," the creature whispered, her silver hair hiding her face. She reached out her white fingers and locked them around Tor Lir's waist. "If I give you my name, will you help?"

"What is your name?"

"Slyvain. I come from the woods. The Master of the Forest woke my tree and took over. He wants the dead to live again and become mortal, with flesh, to gain access to the Beyond."

Questions swirled around Tor Lir's mind and he reached out, caressing Slyvain's cheek. "I am the Nameless One and I have come to help you. But why now? Why do you trust me now?"

Slyvain turned and pointed to the creature roaring in front of the throne. "Because now there is hope."

Letting go of her, Tor Lir crept toward the throne and as he turned to see what caused the creature to roar, he saw Citrine. Her face was ghastly white and blood covered her mouth and chin, dripping onto the forest floor. Her vibrant hair had gone still, turning a gray white as if the life had gone out from it. Bright-red spots glimmered along her hairline and along her neck. As Tor Lir moved toward her, bone-white creatures dropped out of the treetops and a thrashing began in the underbrush.

"Agrim! Now!" Tor Lir shouted as he dashed for the tree where Citrine was tied. Grabbing a knife he'd borrowed from Agrim, he sliced through the rope, setting her free. But Citrine did not move. She sagged more heavily against the tree, her arms pinned behind her back.

Tor Lir dashed around the tree, noticing the Tribe of Fyn shouting out their battle cries as they swung down from hidden perches. Clubs flew and the bone-white creatures shrieked under the assault. The black panthers leaped into the air, ripping vines, limbs, bones, and anything else they could sink their teeth into. Tor Lir wrapped an arm around Citrine's waist and grabbed her hands, cutting them free. Her eyes opened, glazed and unseeing. Her full weight sagged into his arms.

The smell of sulfur increased and Tor Lir backed away from the roaring creatures just as something struck him on the back. He dropped Citrine and tumbled head over heels, his back slamming into the throne. He regained his footing and crouched, realizing how worthless his bow was in such close combat. As he faced the creature, he saw it was the four-legged beast who'd first driven him into the forest. The beast growled and swished its tail, preparing to pounce.

40

WINNER TAKES ALL

ZAUL. CITRINE BLINKED AS HER VISION cleared. She felt Zaul near, but he was still under the grip of the Master and about to attack Tor Lir. It surprised her that Tor Lir had come to her rescue. Her preconceived notions of him drifted away.

Zaul. She tried again as her beast charged Tor Lir. Her ears rang as she pushed her worn body to her knees. Bending over, she spit blood into the dirt and wiped her face with the back of her hand, smearing blood down her arm. Focusing her will, she hurled threads of communication at Zaul, who tore over the ground, teeth glittering in his mouth as he opened them for a bite.

Tor Lir leaped and Zaul missed, but he swung his tail around, smacking trees, the loud sound ringing through the chaos of the battleground.

Zaul. Stop. He is not the enemy. Something broke within her and tears flooded down her face as she saw her beast charge again, ignoring her. *Please, Zaul. Please stop. Come back to me. It's Citrine.*

A rough laugh cut through the air and she felt suspended as if someone had snatched her up by the hair. Citrine screamed, her legs kicking out, although she was still crouched in the mud.

Citrine. This time, the threads of communication were from the Master of the Forest. *You broke through my boundaries, and I sense you stealing back control. You won't earn another life to regret. This is your demise.*

The laugh continued as the Master stood up, stretching out his claws toward Citrine. *You tricked me once. I will not let it happen again.*

Citrine threw up walls in her mind as she scurried away from the terrible hands and height of the Master's fury. His laughter jarred her ears and her head throbbed as she recognized her weakness. Try as she might, she had nothing left to give.

Behind the Master, she saw Zaul strike Tor Lir and a bitter regret poured through her. This was her fault. She should never have gone to Paradise and left her beasts in what she knew was a deadly forest. She was losing them, one by one, because of her selfishness. She wanted a chance to regain her confidence, find herbs, and strike off for a new home, but the enchantment of Paradise held her fast. This was a punishment for her weakness.

Mustering her strength, she closed her eyes and gave it her all just as the ground exploded. A riot of confusion swept through the air and when Citrine opened her eyes, she saw Morag, his eyes blazing citrine as his monstrous, eel-like body, thick as a tree trunk, exploded out of the hole in the ground. His body wrapped around the Master of the Forest and pulled tight, once, then twice. A snapping sound gave way and white bone exploded as Morag twisted the Master. Morag bellowed in rage, a fierceness coming over him, and then as quickly as he'd come, he sank back down, taking the rest of the Master of the Forest with him.

Relief swept through Citrine as the threads of control snapped, setting the bone creatures free. Zaul stopped his attack, wagging his head in confusion. The bone creatures shattered into pieces, and Citrine collapsed. She caught her breath as she lay in the mud while blood trickled down her head and gathered in the corners of her mouth. It was over. They had won. She wondered, briefly, if she would die, for her mind hurt and throbbed as if it would explode. Her fists fell open and her fingers shook as she lay in the muck around the shattered white bone. A faint song began in her heart, and thoughts took her back to her first memory of the land.

She stumbled out of the forest, lame and weary, her heart lifting as Paradise greeted her. Novor Tur-Woodberry skipped over a hill, his merry eyes twinkling at her as he introduced himself. She felt mischief rise in her body, which changed to hope as Novor Tur-Woodberry pressed her hand. He was pure goodness.

Thoughts of chaos faded as he led her to his home, where the

Singing Men danced and the house grew out of nature, welcoming her home to Paradise. She forgot her unhappiness snatched by the incident in the village. She sat down in a chair by the roaring fire and for the first time in her life, she was completely and utterly content.

A sob shook her throat, and a hand lifted her head. Her eyes fluttered open and met emerald green. Concern covered Tor Lir's face as he lifted her in his arms. "You did it." Citrine thought she detected a hint of pride in his voice. "Look at what you have wrought. You saved the forest. You saved Paradise. We can go home."

Citrine lifted her hand and squeezed Tor Lir's shoulder. "I don't know if we saved Paradise. The Master sent his minions there at sunrise. It might be destroyed now."

"We will go see," Tor Lir suggested. "Can you stand?"

Citrine sat up and found Zaul at her side. She threw her arms around him, rubbing her fingers down his rough, scaly back. "I am so sorry," she whispered. "I am so sorry I let you down. I failed you. Never again."

Zaul nuzzled her while black panthers gathered. Citrine saw, in confusion, the waif who'd given her the skull. Citrine stiffened when she saw Agrim and the Tribe of Fyn, but they only nodded at her without a hint of aggression.

"Who are these people?" Citrine looked to Tor Lir.

He smiled, his eyes lighting up oddly. "As I told you. We needed help. This is Agrim's army."

"Are you coming with us to Paradise?" she asked them.

"Only as far as the forest," Agrim announced. "In exchange, you take your beasts from the forest and never let them threaten the cycle of life in the Boundary Line Forest."

Citrine met his dark gaze, understanding his needs as a leader. "I agree."

She sent out feelers through her mind, relieved the voices from the Master and his beasts were gone. *Ava. Grift. Zaul. Morag. It's time to enter Paradise.*

41

GREEN GRASS DYING

Silence hung heavy in the air. The faint call of an owl had been silenced and the whisper of a bird's song came no more to listening ears. The light-hearted jolliness that once embedded the lush hills with hope and merriment had forsaken Paradise. Shards of white bone covered the once green land as Citrine walked with Zaul and Tor Lir out of the Boundary Line Forest. Citrine gasped, a mix of grief and relief swirling through her. Grift and Ava alighted on the blackened ground while Morag's deep voice sounded in her mind. *Banished from our forest . . . hmm . . . shall I meet you where the water turns to jade?*

Are you going to the Jaded Sea?

Aye.

Carry on, Morag, but talk to me often. I need you.

Where there is water, I will find you.

Citrine felt the threads of communication fade and

she turned to Grift, wrapping her arms around his golden neck. His feathers brushed her cheek, and she inhaled, thankful her beasts were with her again and the minions of the Master lay scattered in pieces in Novor Tur-Woodberry's land. However, the blackened ground frightened her, and she swallowed hard, glancing at Tor Lir to see his reaction.

Tor Lir took a step, the black grass and white bone cracking under his feet. The sound echoed in a cadence and faded into the prairie. "Can you still move through portals in the land? Like Novor Tur-Woodberry and his Singing Men?"

Citrine chewed her bottom lip, giving voice to her fears. "No. Not anymore. Where do you think they are? What if they're dead?"

Tor Lir glanced at her. Citrine noticed ever since her battle with the Master, his mannerisms toward her had gentled. He reached out a hand, and she moved away, declining his touch. There was still something odd about him.

Ride me. Grift's suggestion drifted into her mind. *We'll fly over the land and see who's left.*

I flew over the land earlier. Ava joined their conversation. *I saw a shimmering in the middle.*

Citrine felt a sickness in the bottom of her belly. "Tor Lir, we're going to fly."

Ava let Tor Lir mount her back with a sassy remark. *He's beautiful. I'd let him ride me whenever he wants.*

Ava, he's only with us temporarily.

You should keep him. He's wise to your impulsive ways.

Ava.

What? We have to leave anyway—he might prove useful.

I don't want to talk about this right now.

You never want to talk about him.

Ignoring Ava's remark, Citrine swung onto Grift's back, her legs gripping his body, which was slim and muscular like a cat's. He had the head of an eagle-like bird and the body of a lion. Spreading his golden wings, he took off in a run across the land, catching the waves of the wind as he lifted off.

Ava flew above them, stretching her long, serpent-like neck. A cloud of smoke drifted from her nostrils and she snapped at something in the air, catching it between her teeth and swallowing it. Citrine blinked back tears, cursing herself at almost losing her beasts again.

White bone continued to litter the ground as they flew, some including chunks of flesh. The land was silent. Dead. As if no one had ever tread there. When Citrine listened, the song of the land was gone. No more words about Novor Tur-Woodberry and his greatness. The trees seemed dejected. The grass was black and bowed over as if crushed by oppression.

Citrine felt her heart seize and sometime later, her breath caught as she saw a shimmering in the land. It lay in the valley where Novor Tur-Woodberry's thatched cottage used to sit and as they grew closer, a castle appeared in the valley, pointed and round towers shooting off from it. *Ava. Grift. Land here. Zaul, catch up when you can. We are in the middle of the land.*

As they moved into view, a male darted out from the shadow of the valley and dashed away from them.

"Triften!" Citrine shouted as they landed. She tumbled off Grift's back in a manner quite unladylike and ran after the male, waving her arms. "Triften, it's okay, it's me. Citrine!"

"Citrine?" Triften turned around, his eyes glistening with a liquid and his light hair disheveled.

"What happened?" Citrine stopped an arm's length from Triften.

He closed the gap between them, slinging an arm around her shoulder and embracing her.

Citrine kept her arms by her side, her bruises stinging as he touched her. "These bone-white creatures came out of the woods and destroyed everything . . . but what about you? What happened?" Triften's piercing blue eyes stared at her, taking in the smeared blood on her face and arms to the sap still crusted on her hands. He rubbed her shoulders, sympathy appearing on his youthful face.

Citrine frowned, grabbing his arm. "The Master of the Forest is dead, but where is Novor Tur-Woodberry? Where are the people of the land? Are they safe?" She couldn't keep the rising panic out of her voice as her dirty fingernails dug into Triften's arm.

"Most of them, yes. They are at the home of Novor Tur-Woodberry. The onslaught ceased, and the creatures shattered into pieces, but they broke something. The magic of the land is gone. I'm afraid Novor Tur-Woodberry will leave."

"No." Citrine blinked back tears as she let go of Triften and ran to the castle.

An arched doorway flew open and there stood the friendly giant. The merriment in his eyes was gone and his face held a weathered and somber look about it. "Citrine," he rumbled in his deep voice. A great sorrow filled her, and she felt as if she were treading water with nowhere to go, slowly sinking.

She covered the distance in a matter of seconds, sinking to her knees in front of Novor Tur-Woodberry. She folded her fingers into his hand and brought it to her cheek, inhaling his scent of all that was great and good in the world. "Novor Tur-Woodberry. I beg your forgiveness. This is my fault. The Master of the Forest exerted his control over me and I did not stop it until it was too late. But please, tell me, can you fix this? Will you stay and make the land whole again? I will help. I will do anything. Just please, please don't leave me."

"My dear." Novor Tur-Woodberry placed a hand on her head like a blessing before he lifted her chin up, forcing her to meet his eyes. "As I told you before, my time has come. It is time to say goodbye."

"No. Please." Citrine felt the tears brim over in her eyes, but he held her gaze. "Please don't leave. We aren't ready. *I'm* not ready for something new. I need you." A sob burst from her throat and she held her breath, trying to force it away. A rush of wind filled the air, but Citrine kept her eyes on Novor Tur-Woodberry as if she could hold him there. Her heart beat with desperation to save him and to save the land.

"Listen." Novor Tur-Woodberry wiped the tears from her eyes with the pads of his fingers. He caressed the map of her face as he spoke. "There is nothing you can do to stop this, but the Creator has brought you a companion, Tor Lir, and the wind lady has brought a gift to the land. I will not say, 'Do not grieve,' for grief is healing. But our time together, no matter how short, has ended. It is time for the cleansing winds to blow and then I will take my leave."

Citrine squeezed his hand and let her bitter tears flow over them. She shook her head, knowing there was nothing she could do, yet desiring to stop it all the same. The heavy feeling in her gut was the knowledge that it was all her fault. Her actions had driven Novor Tur-Woodberry away and destroyed his land. It was a heavy guilt to live with, and even all the fighting she'd done could not make it right.

"Don't blame yourself." Novor Tur-Woodberry pulled her up. "Come, stand beside me, and watch what will take place."

A gust blew over her and Novor Tur-Woodberry. She nodded at his words, although nothing he said would take the guilt away in her heart. Brushing away her tears, although she knew they would flow again, she watched as a lady and a child appeared out of the wind.

The child looked to be about ten years of age and had long dark hair and skin as brown as a nut. She smiled, showing off her white teeth as she flew out of the breeze to Novor Tur-Woodberry. Placing her hands palms together, she bowed her head, her silky black hair cascading around her shoulders. She blinked, her eyelashes sweeping toward the ruined ground. "Novor Tur-Woodberry, my mother bade me come to you with the gift of wind. If you give your blessing, I will sweep this land from the abomination of beasts and leave no traces of the great evil that befell it."

"You have my blessing, daughter of wind," Novor Tur-Woodberry rumbled.

The child smiled again and, turning, she ran to her mother, grabbed her hand, and let the winds blow.

Citrine watched through tears as the wind picked up, taking the wind lady and her daughter and creating a cyclone. The shards of white bone whipped up in the wind as it moved over the land. Everywhere it touched wiped clean as if the Master of the Forest and his beasts had never entered the land of Novor Tur-Woodberry.

"Now what happens?" Citrine whispered as she stood beside Novor Tur-Woodberry, resting her head on his chest. "Can you stay?"

Triften and Tor Lir walked up to the castle and sat on the doorstep below them, watching, while Grift and Ava took to the skies, following the wind as if it were a game.

"Tell me what happened in the wood," Novor Tur-Woodberry said instead.

Citrine watched Tor Lir lift his face, meeting her eyes. His emerald gaze was emotionless, yet he nodded as if encouraging her to speak. Trading off, they relayed the story of entering the wood, meeting the Tribe of Fyn, and defeating the Master of the Forest and his beasts. Citrine noticed Triften lifted his head to watch her from time to time, and she wondered if this would become one story he told over and over again. A quiet warning rose in her heart because she wanted no one to know she was the Enchantress and controlled rare, mythical beasts.

"You have done well." Novor Tur-Woodberry nodded at Citrine and Tor Lir. "Do not worry about what happened here. Citrine, I have something to show you."

He turned to the door of his home and waved his hand. A shimmering appeared in the air and the white orb appeared, suspended in the archway. Reaching out, Novor Tur-Woodberry lay his hand on it, and a picture appeared. Looking into it, Citrine saw the land of Novor Tur-Woodberry. It appeared like a replica with the rolling hills and cottages perched on hilltops with smoke rolling out of chimneys.

"It's your land. But I don't understand?"

"The Silver-White Heart captured a replica of my land within it and saved the people who escaped the rampage of the beasts. Once I expelled the darkness inside the Silver-White Heart, I brought it to my home, this castle."

"You mean everything is okay?" Citrine felt a spark of hope in her heart, like a light beam in a dark room.

"Yes, but I must leave and all those who remain on my land may come with me."

Citrine opened her mouth to ask, but the words died on her lips and she understood. She was not welcome in this new land. "Will I ever see you again?" she asked.

"The opening to my land may appear from time to time to weary travelers," Novor Tur-Woodberry mused. "But evil will never touch this land."

A song rose in the air as the orb drifted back into the home of Novor Tur-Woodberry, allowing the Singing Men to perch on the doorstep. Their voices blended in a harmonic tune, a bittersweet song of goodbye ringing out as the wind cured the land from the scourge of evil.

"It is time." Novor Tur-Woodberry lifted his hands and took a step back.

42

FADE FROM VIEW

TOR LIR STOOD BACK AS THE BEASTS FLEW overhead. Grift's golden wings caught rays of the green light in the sky while Ava's deep blue feathers added a richness to the colors dancing in the wind. The castle of Novor Tur-Woodberry shimmered. The winds blew around it and when he glanced across the land, he saw the shards of white bone had vanished and white flowers had grown in a matter of seconds, too quick for his eyes to see. They bloomed across the land, sending a sweet scent into his nostrils.

What was once lush and green was now white prairie, like a bride on the day she took a mate. He recalled the white petals and golden liquor from the celebrations the Iaens had, with sweet songs and whimsical music as they wished the couple an enchanting life together.

A shudder shook the ground. Zaul growled and

swished his tail as he stood beside Citrine. Tor Lir flinched each time he looked at the creature, understanding its mind was no longer possessed but recalling the dissatisfying feeling of being attacked. Citrine lifted her head and tears flowed down her face, her odd eyes clouded in a haze of sorrow.

Tor Lir felt something like emotion touch his heart, and he shook himself. He recalled his words to the green giantess. *I do not love, and therefore I will not destroy the world because of love . . . I am not swayed by emotion.*

He watched the people of the land flood out of the castle, lifting their arms and shouting bittersweet words to each other. Triften and Citrine wove around the people, embracing, laughing, and crying with them as they said goodbye. A multitude of children with long light hair shouted in merriment as they recanted their trials and tribulations when the bone creatures attacked.

Tor Lir crossed his arms as understanding washed over him. He understood why emotion moved mortals and why they loved each other. A knowing sat heavy on his heart and a tune rushed through his mind. *Long may you live. Long may you prosper.* He brushed the words away, a fear thudding in his heart. They had restored the balance; he felt it in his bones, but it was time to move on, time to leave.

Another quake shook the ground and Tor Lir closed his eyes, searching for the threads of imbalance. There was nothing but peace. But the forests of Shimla were still too close, and he wanted to leave the Eastern Hill

Countries of the South World behind and pass into the west where there was no such thing as Daygone. A deep sensation of fear began in the pit of his stomach, and he wavered where he stood until a hand touched his shoulder.

"Tor Lir, look."

Opening his eyes, he saw Citrine stood by his side, traces of tears still on her face. She pointed up at the castle. The winds rocked it out of the ground and somehow it lifted as if it had wings of a great beast. The castle floated upward as gently as a feather on the updraft of the wind. Suddenly, the glass windows of the house flew open, and the faces of the people of the land appeared, waving at them. Citrine lifted her hands and waved, a sudden smile coming to her face, curving her cheeks up and back. The wind blew her vibrant hair, and she looked like an enchantress, ready to call upon the world to do her biding.

The castle doors opened and Novor Tur-Woodberry and his Singing Men appeared with a song on their lips. The words weaved a harmonious tune as if a thousand creatures were singing them. They sang of the greatness of Novor Tur-Woodberry and his enchanted land, and how those weary of traveling and life might again find the passage to the hidden realm of Novor Tur-Woodberry.

Prisms of emerald and gold shot through the air, like falling stars, gracing the castle with a hidden glimpse of enchanted purity and joy. Then, like stars winking out, one by one, a shimmering hung in the air, much like the one Tor Lir had seen when he first visited the home of Novor Tur-Woodberry. The top most parts of the castle faded into the clouds, and little by little the entire castle faded from view as if it had never been. The only things that remained were the song in the air and the sweet fragrance from the white flowers.

"Whenever you see white flowers and hear the song in the air, you'll know you're close to entering the hidden land of Novor Tur-Woodberry," Triften whispered.

Tor Lir eyed him, for he could not recall meeting the male before. Triften's blue eyes had a lost look to them, as if he wished for something he could not obtain. He noticed Tor Lir looking at him and turned, a light in his eyes as the winds faded away with the castle. "I'm Triften the Storyteller."

Tor Lir gave him a nod to acknowledge he'd heard him but said nothing else.

"Now this is an exciting tale, one I have not had for many years," Triften mused. "I must tell others what I have seen and heard here. Citrine, where are you going now?"

"I don't know." Citrine was quiet, her eyes roving back and forth as she watched her beasts. Tor Lir wondered if she were speaking to them.

"Citrine?" Tor Lir called her attention away from the beasts. "Will you come with me?"

"Me?" Citrine dropped a hand over her heart and gave him a wry look as if she did not believe his request.

Tor Lir smirked, watching the way her eyes widened and nostrils flared. "Aye. I thought we did well in the forest; besides, it will be much easier to keep an eye on your mischief if you come with me."

"I promised my beasts a home—"

"And you haven't found it yet." Tor Lir slid his eyes over to examine Triften, wondering what the storyteller knew of Citrine's true power. "You cause many things, and I need you to come with me. At some point, I promise I will find a home fit for you and your beasts, where you will not riot on the freedom of others."

"Promises." Citrine's lips curved upward. "I do not believe in promises. Where will you go?"

"Wherever I am needed. I go where there is mischief."

Citrine smiled, although traces of sorrow stayed in her eyes. "I don't know where else to go. I will go with you until a better offer is given."

"Aye then, that is enough for me." Tor Lir felt a sensation of relief.

Citrine turned to Triften, who was staring at the beasts in the sky above, his finger pointing up. "Will you come with us?"

Triften's hand came down, his mouth open as he glanced at Citrine. "Your beasts?" He stared.

"Will you come with us?" Citrine repeated.

"For a night or two," he agreed. "Tell me the story

again, so I may remember it. Tell me what happened in the forest and of these beasts you speak of."

"It's a wild story," Citrine said. "Others may not believe it."

"The world is fresh and young," Triften disagreed. "People believe in everything."

"Come on then," Tor Lir called as he strode through the white flowers.

When he glanced back, he saw Citrine staring at the place where Novor Tur-Woodberry's castle had faded, and the song of the land whispered through the wind.

43

A NEW QUEST

Triften rolled up his bedroll and gave Citrine his best smile, one that imparted hope and health. He'd walked with Citrine and Tor Lir through the white flowers for two days as new life rolled into the meadow. Yellow butterflies flittered through the air and the songs of the birds gave life to the meadow. New trees sprouted up, growing at an uncanny speed.

Triften nodded at Tor Lir, the nameless one, trying to keep from staring at the odd male. His emerald-green eyes reminded Triften of someone he'd lost.

Alarm bells rang in his mind as he told Citrine and Tor Lir goodbye. It was time for him to go to the annual gathering of the Disciples of Ithar, and this time he had a tale for them. Excitement made his fingers shake as he adjusted the bedroll on his back.

It would surprise the disciples to find the new breed had risen and was already at large. Triften could not believe his fortune. He would be the one to bring life-changing news to the disciples. It had been a long time since he'd had an adventure in his nomadic life. Once the decree concerning the new breed went forth, he would have a reason and purpose for living once again.

As he set off toward the fortress on the eastern end of the land, he glanced back once more to confirm his knowledge. Tor Lir and Citrine stood on a hill, the sun in their faces as they walked west. He saw Citrine's shadow as she held her hands out, running her fingers through the white blossoms. He shuddered, recalling the parchment he'd taken from her cottage. Hidden mysteries surrounded her, but it was Tor Lir who frightened him. He did not have a shadow.

Dear Readers,

Thank you for reading *Realm of Beasts*.

If you loved the book and have a minute to spare, I would truly appreciate a brief review on the site where you bought the book. It can be short, so don't worry about trying to sound too eloquent.

Leave a Review:

Amazon

Goodreads

Tor Lir and Citrine will return in *Realm of Mortals*.

If you're curious about the war between the mortals and immortals, read the series that started it all.

The Complete Four Worlds Series (Books 1–4)

The Five Warriors

The Blended Ones

Myran: A Tale of the Four Worlds

Eliesmore and the Green Stone

Eliesmore and the Jeweled Sword

ACKNOWLEDGMENTS

The writing of this story would not have happened without readers—in particular, Lana Turner, who asked for a tale about Novor Tur-Woodberry.

I'm also truly grateful for the people who never cease to support and encourage my work, including my four sisters, my parents, and the many authors I work with.

Special thanks goes to Shayla Raquel for polishing this story and to Amalia Chitulescu for creating a gorgeous cover with a lovely view of Paradise.

Finally, to all fans of the Four Worlds: if you have a story suggestion or characters and creatures you'd like to read about in future books, email me:
angela@angelajford.com.

ABOUT THE AUTHOR

Angela J. Ford is an award-winning blogger and author of the international bestselling epic fantasy series, The Four Worlds. She enjoys traveling, hiking, and can often be found with her nose in a book.

Aside from writing, she enjoys the challenge of working with marketing technology and builds websites for authors. She is currently working on her next epic fantasy series: Legend of the Nameless One.

If you happen to be in Nashville, you'll most likely find her at a local coffee shop, enjoying a white chocolate mocha and furiously working on her next book.

facebook.com/angelajfordauthor
twitter.com/aford21
instagram.com/aford21

Printed in Great Britain
by Amazon